DOE AND THE WOLF

Furry United Coalition #5

EVE LANGLAIS

Copyright © October 2013, Eve Langlais

Cover Art © Dreams 2 Media

Produced in Canada

http://www.EveLanglais.com

All Rights Reserved

Doe and the Wolf is a work of fiction and the characters, events and dialogue found within the story are of the author's imagination and are not to be construed as real. Any resemblance to actual events or persons, either living or deceased, is completely coincidental.

No part of this book may be reproduced or shared in any form or by any means, electronic or mechanical, including but not limited to digital copying, file sharing, audio recording, email and printing without permission in writing from the author.

eBook ISBN: 978-1-927459-44-7

Print ISBN: 978-1-77384-033-8

PROLOGUE

"You're firing me?" Damn. There went his plans to buy a bigger television.

"I'm sorry, Everett, but you've left us no choice. As of this moment, you are no longer a recognized agent of this bureau, and you need to relinquish your FUC badge."

No, not his badge! That shiny emblem was the ultimate panty dropper. "But I solved the case!" Shouldn't he be receiving a medal instead of the shaft? As usual, he unraveled the clues, caught his animal and, once he hit his favorite hotspot, would get the girl—for one night of naked, sweaty fun. *Awooo!*

"Solved it, yes, while putting dozens at risk of serious injury. You also destroyed public property and almost caused a media relations nightmare by allowing a human to spot you shifting. Not to mention, you displayed a gross disregard for the orders you were given asking you to stand down and wait for backup."

His boss held up fingers as she ticked off the problems with his methods. She held up quite a few.

"Waiting would have meant them getting away." And if there was something Everett hated, it was watching criminals slip through his paws. *I also love the chase, the more mayhem the merrier.* But he didn't think mentioning that would help his case.

"Better we catch them later than suffer the consequences of your maverick actions." Kloe, head of the FUC department in this city, shut his folder and leaned back in her chair with a heavy sigh. "I don't disagree this decision sucks. Just so you know, I tried to get the council to place you on administrative leave. You're a good agent. A bit rash and perhaps less than delicate in your dealings, but you get results. Unfortunately, given your history,"—she eyed his thick file with a pointed stare—"they felt it best for the shifter community at large that you no longer be involved as an active agent of the FUC office."

"This is bullshit." Also, possibly fallout from the girl he'd recently dumped whose daddy held a lofty position high up in the ASS chain. Not one of his brightest decisions. His da always did say, "Don't poach where you shit." Of course, his father meant it literally, but the analogy still fit.

"I am sorry, Everett. With your skills, though, you should have no problem picking up some work as a security guard or something."

"A security guard!" His voice hit a high pitch of incredulity that made him pop a few whiskers in agitation. "You're talking to a former Marine."

"Key word being former. As I recall, you got discharged for being unable to obey orders."

"I did survival skills training at Quantico."

"Before they kicked you out for not listening to the instructors. Are you starting to see a pattern?"

Yeah. He did. He needed to stop working with people who thought the law and criminals should abide by a strict set of rules. How many thugs would have slipped away had he followed protocols to the T? How many more victims would there be today if he stood around waiting, while some soft-bellied idiot in a suit twiddled his thumbs in an office waiting for the paperwork to come through? *That's not how I work.* Which in turn led to him being out of a job. Again.

Grumbling, he slid his FUC badge across the scarred desktop. He'd miss the symbol, not just because of the paycheck and benefits, but because he'd truly enjoyed working for FUC. The Furry United Coalition made him feel he was doing something to help his fellow shifters. It gave him a sense of purpose.

Where else would he find a job that would pay him to let loose the hunter inside him?

The slaps of commiseration from his fellow agents did nothing to dispel his gloom and neither did the several drafts of beer he downed at a local bar. He didn't drink for long, not at five bucks a glass. Grabbing a case of beer, he headed for home where he could marinate in the injustice of his dismissal.

Fired! He still had a hard time wrapping his head around it. After all he'd done and achieved. How could they toss him out like that? Sure, he could have perhaps tempered his actions and not engaged the weasel until he'd cleared the propane station. Just like he could have taken a look around before shifting. In his defense, the homeless man in his cardboard box of a home who'd seen him morph wasn't the most reliable of eye-witness accounts. But no one listened. FUC screwed him over, without lube and without a care.

Unemployed with no skills other than that of a cop and ex soldier, what could he do? His severance package would only last so long. The idea of returning to a mundane job lacking the excitement and thrill of detective work didn't appeal. And it wasn't as if he could use his FUC credentials to get himself hired by the human authorities. Besides, did he really want to work under some pencil pushing human?

Flipping on his television, he sulked in his La-Z-Boy chair, channel surfing until he came across an action show involving some dude with a mullet wearing sunglasses chasing someone down a dirty alley. It took him a few minutes to realize he wasn't watching fiction but a reality show called *Dog, The Bounty Hunter*.

Does this guy actually get paid to chase and take into custody bail jumpers? He straightened in his seat, his interest piqued. When the show ended, Everett hopped on to his laptop and did some Google searching. Not only were bounty hunters—who also went by the lofty title of fugitive recovery agents—paid to go after bad guys who tried to evade punishment, they did so without many of the restrictions he'd faced in an office environment. The icing on the cake, though? Dog got to wear cool freaking clothes and keep his hair as long as he liked.

I could do that job. Of course, he didn't have an

awesome mullet like that Dog fellow, but he did have a wicked pair of sideburns to rival that movie fellow, Wolverine. He also looked great in a pair of leather pants—not the real thing because he didn't believe in using animal products as clothing unless he'd hunted and skinned it himself.

Goodbye and good riddance to FUC. Hello, Lone Wolf Agency. Huffing and puffing criminals back where they belonged, behind bars.

1

Years later...

With a mighty leap, Everett cleared the hood of the car in hot pursuit of his target. The bail jumper might have youth and agility on his side, but Everett was a pro, and a champion jumper. Those agility training classes, where he'd played the part of dog, had really paid off when it came to honing his skills. It was getting his shots at the vet so he could sign up for classes that sucked. No one, not even a paid doc for animals, should *ever* put fingers, gloved or not, in the places this one dared. She was lucky she didn't lose her digits for the affront. As for the friend who played the part of his owner? After Tom finished trying to kill himself via laughter, he almost died until he swore he'd never reveal the indignity.

So it was with confidence and grace, Everett's wolf, wearing a collar and tags to promote his guise of trained service dog, tangled himself in the legs of the fleeing criminal and tripped him. The runner hit the ground and Everett pounced on his chest. A low growl and bared teeth sufficed to keep the male from moving as he blubbered, "Nice doggy. Don't eat me." As if he'd ruin his palate on scum.

Tom, his handler, arrived panting, partially hunched over, a hand on his hip to brace himself. "Everett, I swear to God, I am going to kill you one day, if you don't manage to kill me first." No, the extra large fries Tom kept ordering for lunch would. As his best friend, Everett was just doing his part to keep Tom in shape.

He lolled his tongue and winked, since talking in front of the human would probably get him in trouble.

Tom grimaced. "Don't you give me that face. I am too old for this."

"Yeah, and if you know what's good for you, gramps, you'll let me go," the thug lying underneath Everett threatened.

A lifted lip and a rumbling snarl shut him up. Everett trotted off to the side as Tom zip tied their bounty's hands together and marched him back to their SUV.

Another successful hunt by the LWA, short for the Lone Wolf Agency. They didn't have their own television show yet, but all the cop shops knew, if someone slipped their bail, who to call for help. *Awooo!*

After they'd gotten their perp booked and the paperwork filled out to receive their check, they headed back to their office, also known as his garage. Downtown space came at a monthly premium and, given they spent as little time as possible in an office, proved neither worth it nor necessary. So long as they had a filing cabinet and a computer, they could call anywhere their office, even his cluttered garage. If it was good enough for the IRS, then it was good enough for LWA. Not to mention a short commute in the morning.

Only once the metal roll down door had hummed shut did Everett morph from his wolf into himself. As he grabbed his pants from the pile he'd left behind, Tom continued to grumble.

"Why must they always run? Would it be so hard for them to just stand still and hold out their hands?"

"But then how would we get our exercise?"

A dirty look from his partner made Everett chuckle.

Tom continued to complain. "I'm a sloth. Our idea of exercise involves climbing a tree to find a good branch to nap on."

"You're no fun."

"And you're insane."

"It's why we work well together," Everett replied with a toothy grin.

Tom shook his head. "Why me?"

Why indeed? Unlike Everett, Tom played well with others. He went to work on time. Did his job and never rocked any boats, yet when Everett had called his old friend and told him he was contemplating starting his own business as a bounty hunter, Tom quit his job as an accountant and declared himself his sidekick.

It had worked out better than expected. Given Everett's wolf side was best for tracking fugitives, they came up with a clever plan. When they caught a suspect's scent or ferretted out a location, Everett shifted into his wolf either in the garage or, if in the field, behind the dark-tinted glass of their company truck. He acted as Tom's canine helper, albeit a really big one. Tom got perverse pleasure out of introducing him as his oversized, king-sized German shepherd. Those who knew their breeds questioned the designation, but for the most part, humans accepted the explanation, and no one made a big deal, so long as Everett didn't maul—too badly—the suspects he took down.

"So how much was this guy worth?"

Not anything close enough to get himself the brand new dream truck—fully loaded with GPS, a kick ass sound system and heated seats—he was eyeing over at the dealership, but it would pay his utility bills and mortgage for the month. Bounty hunting, while fun, was hard work. Yes, it could pay, but how much really depended on the skipper. It definitely wasn't a steady paycheck. Not all criminals chose to run out before their court dates, but still, Everett loved the adrenaline rush that came with the job.

Speaking of which, the fax machine hummed. *Excellent.* It looked like a new assignment was coming down the wire. The paper was still warm when Everett snagged the bulletin as it spat out of his printer. His brows lifted as he noted the header then lifted higher when he read the content of the fax.

"Dude, check this out." He handed the sheet to Tom.

Not given to extreme emotional outbursts, even the stoic Tom whistled. "I'll be damned. They must be desperate if they're asking you for help."

The who in question was his old FUC employer.

To the attention of Everett Johnson, Fugitive Recovery Agent of the Lone Wolf Agency

As you may be aware, there was an incident a while back with a certain rodent involved in experimentation. While the wily mammal in question was dealt with, some of its involuntary companions escaped custody. While a large number have been apprehended or accounted for, it has come to our attention that a certain violent predator has been spotted in your area. Despite your lack of agent status, we would like to hire your services in tracking and eliminating the creature currently terrorizing the campers at your nearby national park. You will of course be suitably rewarded.

The possibility exists that more than one suspected animal is in the park. Use extreme caution. The subjects are considered armed and extremely dangerous.

Sincerely,
FUC Management

"Hot damn. They must really be overworked if they're asking you for help," Tom said after he finished reading aloud the missive, his tone rife with disbelief.

"They've got a lot of nerve, that's for sure." Bitter? Him? Darned straight he was. Getting fired, while a good thing in the end for his paycheck, still rankled.

"You going to give them a hand? Or tell them to shove it where the sun don't shine?"

"And pass up a chance not only for money but a great big middle finger on their mistake in letting me go? Hell no. I'll capture their escaped woodland creature. I mean, did you see the list of suspects? A deer, a cat, a gecko, and an ostrich, just to name a few. Piece of freaking bacon. I'm a wolf. We serve these animals as appetizers at family get-togethers."

Funny how fate had a way of making a wolf eat his words.

Less than a week after getting the fax, Everett wished he'd not acted so cocky and that he'd gotten more information. Reading that the animals he was chasing were a little different due to some experimentation did not prepare a man to meet the monstrous thing face to face.

A gecko should not tower eight feet tall with six-inch fangs or possess claws sharp enough to slice and dice his carcass into hairy julienne fries. As if to add insult to injury, no one had mentioned the bloodlust this creature suffered from, a slavering madness not usually seen outside of horror movies.

I should have brought a gun. But, oh no, he preferred the paws-on approach.

Scuttling through the low underbrush, Everett's wolf form blended well with the shadows, but it didn't prevent the mutant gecko from tracking him with ease, knocking aside branches and saplings as if they were mere matchsticks in its path.

Goddamn. What kind of steroids was this thing fed to make it so big? Injured, and limping along on three legs, Everett couldn't outrun it, and he'd lost Tom a few miles back. The sloth couldn't keep up, and a good thing too. Tom wouldn't stand a chance against this oversized lizard, which, despite evolution and what online sources claimed, could run on two or four legs.

Bursting from the edge of the forest, Everett skidded to a halt, the sharp drop-off of a bluff signaling the end of this path. *Just freaking great.* He whipped around as the crashing of branches and underbrush drew closer. And closer.

What to do? He couldn't fly—and he wasn't Wile E. Coyote to jump off the cliff holding a sign saying *Help!* He bore no weapons save his teeth and claws, which did some damage against the leathery skin of the behemoth hunting him, just not enough to stop it. Bad odds or not, he wouldn't go down cowering. Even if he didn't stand a chance, he'd do his damnedest and fight.

The stench of his opponent reached him a moment before it appeared. Jaws open wide in a slobbering grin, the lime green gecko with gray splotches lumbered on two legs from the woods, its stubby front arms waving. *All the better to grab me with.*

Everett switched back to his human form and tried diplomacy—something he'd flunked when in school. "I don't suppose we could discuss this?"

"Urgle. Muaha, blerg."

While he couldn't decipher the words, Everett deemed the razor-tipped claws that reached for him a definitive no. He dove out of the way, rolling as he hit the ground and coming up with a stray tree limb. He swung it. *Thunk.* He managed a solid blow against the monster's side, which had absolutely no effect.

The creature grasped at his staff and yanked it from his grip, a big bully taking away his toy. Not good. Then he lunged at Everett, who tried to dodge; however, his injured leg buckled at the sudden movement, and the gecko got a hold of him.

Wrestling on the edge of the precipice, Everett stared

into the face of death, and damn was it ugly—not to mention in dire need of some dental floss.

I do believe I see some campers stuck between his front teeth.

As his rib cage compressed in a hug, he couldn't escape, and his eyesight blurred, Everett continued to struggle; however, the only things he could move were his legs. Everett wasn't one to discount a dirty shot when his life depended on it. Up came his knee, right into the fleshy area between the thing's legs.

What do you know, he'd found a vulnerable spot. With a bellow of pain, the monster let go. A good thing in most circumstances, but as Everett plunged down, down, down, the ground receding above him, he managed to utter one final, "Ah, hell. I wish I'd learned to swim."

But that proved a moot point because as soon as he hit the water, head first, he blacked out.

2

Her furry ears twitched and she paused in her grazing. *What was that?*

The usual noises of the forest died down. Something spooked the wildlife. But what? And more importantly, should she flee or investigate?

Could be nothing. It didn't take much to send the less evolved wildlife that lived in these parts into hiding. Taking a few ginger steps toward the edge of the forest, she strained to hear what spooked them.

Dawn heard the distinctive groan before she saw the body. He was splayed on the shore, a naked, muddy mess. Her first instinct was to run, dash into the safety of the forest and hide. Running a year ago would have saved her the nightmare of captivity. But her tender nature, then and now, saw her picking her way daintily across the slick stones lining the river's edge.

As if sensing her approach, the injured man raised his head and muttered a very distinctive, "Fuck."

Eep! Instinct took over, and she trotted back to the

safety of the forest. She huddled behind a tree, holding her breath and listening. No sound of pursuit. Peering around the edge of the trunk, she noted he laid where she'd left him, on his stomach now, unconscious again, a helpless victim and an easy feast for the predators who lived within the woods.

Not her problem.

He groaned again.

Stupid. Stupid. Stupid. Her subconscious kept repeating it over and over, yet she couldn't help herself from approaching the large, soaked form washed up on the shore, the coppery scent of blood perfuming the air. Stupid of her or not, her grandmother had raised her to always lend a helping hoof. It would have been nice if that hoof came with a stretcher.

Eyeing the body on the ground, Dawn wasn't quite sure what to do. On the one hand, the stranger was in obvious need of assistance. The numerous contusions and gashes that bled all over his nude body screamed, *"Requires medical attention now!"* However, at the same time, the man was a predator, a Lycan to be exact, or so her twitching nose claimed. There was something inherently wrong about a doe helping a wolf.

Or there would be, if this were still the dark ages before the shifter council had formed and outlawed the hunting of weaker sentient breeds. Still...*I am supposed to be hiding.* Hiding from the humans. Hiding from her own kind. And, most especially, hiding from FUC, the agency that first promised to help her, then, because of a miscalculation on their part, issued orders to terminate her.

Is it my fault I'm a little different?

Lamenting over her fate didn't solve her current dilemma. Help the wolf or let him die? That was what it boiled down to. She knew what her mother and father would say; however, Dawn had left home to escape their archaic ways. With a heavy sigh, Dawn shifted, and hoped the male would have the decency to ignore her nudity if he happened to regain consciousness. She bent at the knees, grabbed a hold of him under the armpits, and heaved.

He didn't budge, not even a quarter of an inch.

Hmm. That didn't bode well. She thought of fetching her first aid kit and patching him up on the shore, but the forest noises made by stirring predators, some of them daring to come closer because they scented weakness and blood, changed her mind. Even if she did bandage the male where he lay, she couldn't leave him defenseless and comatose.

Time to put her Girl Scout badges to use, that and some of her newly acquired skills, courtesy of one demented mastermind intent on ruling the world. Thankfully, that plan was foiled, but the results lingered. But would they work on something so large?

She regarded the injured male, a finger tapping her chin. Definitely taller than her petite five-foot-three stature and heavier than her chubby one-hundred-and-fifty-pound frame. His body wasn't overly muscled, but it was well toned, his arms thick with muscle and his thighs corded as well. She couldn't have said if he was handsome or not. His longish hair masked his features, along with streaks of blood and mud. Studying him was well and good, but it didn't help to get him to safety.

But how am I supposed to do it alone? Or more accurately, how could she accomplish her task without tapping into her other half, her mutated half?

She sighed. Since her rebirth at the hands of the mastermind, Dawn had discovered some interesting side effects. Most of them involved physical changes to her once delicate and gentle doe side, changes she preferred not to dwell on. However, there was one thing that might prove handy, a new special ability that she could draw upon while human even. Telekinesis. She could move things with her mind, well, little things at least as far as she knew. She'd never tried with anything bigger than a coffee cup, this new aspect a recent and frightening power to someone who'd only ever aspired to a normal life.

All I ever wanted was a husband, kids, and a white picket fence in the suburbs. Instead, she'd ended up a fugitive from her own kind, could shapeshift into Frankendoe and, like an X-Man, or X-Girl, could move things if she concentrated hard enough.

Clenching her fists and gritting her teeth, she stared at the wolf, willing him to rise. He remained slumped. Fudge on a stick. *Don't tell me my powers are gone.* For some reason, the moment brought to mind *Star Wars* and a scene where Luke was bitching to Yoda that he couldn't lift his starcruiser because it was too big. *Feel the force, Dawn.* And don't giggle.

Determined, she concentrated harder, and the stranger's body trembled. She dug her nails into her palms and willed him up, and yes, he rose!

Back she inched, sweat pearling on her brow as she hovered him from the stream's edge to the firmer ground of the embankment. She managed about six feet before he dropped, her trembling frame unable to retain the concentration needed. Not far enough.

Drained, she slumped to the ground. This wasn't going to work, not when the cabin and her supplies remained a few hundred yards away still. Since she lacked the power to move him with her telekinesis, she resorted to using her brain. No matter which way she puzzled it, she needed some supplies, so, like it or not, she needed to leave him alone for a few minutes. Back she shifted into her doe—because naked streaking women in the woods tended to garnish attention. On four agile, overly large hooves, she ran to her hiding spot where she fetched an old blanket and some rope. Returning just as quick, she breathed a sigh of relief to find him untouched and where she'd left him. Despite her fatigue from all the shifting, and the use of her power, she once again took to her human shape. She constructed a stretcher using two long, fairly straight branches with the fabric lashed between them. She then created a harness of sorts.

Using her telekinesis, Dawn dredged deep and found enough mental juice left to heave him onto her makeshift stretcher. Then, she called forth her doe. Without hands, it proved a little tricky to guide the rope halter over her head and around her neck, but she managed. Then, like a packhorse, she dragged and pulled home her riverside find, to do what with she didn't know. But, despite what her new feral side suggested, she wasn't about to have him for dinner basted in barbecue sauce. Or keep his fur as a rug.

3

Out she ventured from the edge of the woods with dainty steps that still crushed the foliage underfoot. Bleary-eyed, Everett tried to make sense of what he saw, but couldn't, his injuries too great. One thing he did know was his mind was not working at full speed because what Everett saw made no sense, and blinking didn't make it any better. He must have whacked his head good.

He tried to speak, or at least let the creature know who he worked for and who to call for help. He croaked a feeble, "FUC."

The timid creature recoiled and bounded back into the forest.

A groan left him as he realized he'd probably just tried to speak with a plain old woodland creature. It seemed his sense of smell was shot, along with his poor body. That didn't bode well.

Half in, half out of the water, he managed to roll to his stomach and claw his way farther up the muddy embankment, a few inches of torture that left him panting.

Black spots danced before his eyes. He could feel the dark nirvana hovering over him, waiting to grab him in its embrace. He needed to fight it. Needed to...

The next time he woke, which surprised him greatly, he did so under a wooden slatted roof on a bed covered in a blanket, which smelled oddly enough of lilacs. He knew the scent because his mother liked to grow them when he was boy on the farm. He could still hear his father grumble about the darned things taking up valuable farmland space, but despite that, he allowed them just because they made his mother smile.

Do the lilacs mean I'm home? No. Because home had white plaster ceilings, and the mincing steps approaching did not belong to his mother. Not to mention, his mother had never tied him to a bed.

What the hell is going on? He pulled at his bonds, but the rope held him in a kinky, spread-eagle pose that he might have enjoyed more if he thought it meant pleasure. But, given the way his body ached, he doubted he'd gotten kidnapped by a gorgeous woman intent on seducing his body. Although, the soft tread of steps approaching did seem to indicate someone of the female persuasion.

Shutting his eyes, he tried to feign sleep, but whoever approached didn't believe his sham, that or they were naturally nervous because they inched so slowly and tentatively he almost growled at them to hurry it up. When the feather-light touch came on his brow, he couldn't help a bark of surprise, though.

The woman took flight, and despite opening his

eyes as quickly as possible, he caught only a fleeting glimpse of long brown hair trailing behind her as she fled the room.

But she couldn't hide the sweet roundness of her ass or her scent.

A doe. A deer. A female deer. Everett couldn't help a most wolfish grin. Of all the luck. *I'm alive, healing, and I think I just found one of the missing FUC fugitives.* Or, more accurately, she'd found him.

The day was looking up. As for his current predicament involving rope and the possibility he was in the hands of a serial killer?

Minor details. After all, he'd prevailed against the PIG Gang–Porcines in the Ghetto—beaten the Hood, and put Grandma Red—so named because of her penchant for spitting red cherry pits when she tortured her rivals—in shifter jail where she belonged. What did he have to fear from one little woman?

"Little doe, little doe," he called. "Won't you come in?"

Slender fingers curled around the doorframe, and big brown eyes peered in. "Will you promise not to eat me?"

"Oh, I'd love to *eat* you," he said in a husky voice with a naughty wink that usually worked wonders with the ladies.

"Eep!" With a squeak, she ducked out of sight.

What the hell? Surely she didn't take his words literally? Couldn't she tell he flirted with her? When she didn't reappear, he yelled, "Just kidding."

Cautiously, she leaned back in, her expression that

of a distrusting animal ready to bolt. "So you won't make a meal out of me?"

Laughter barked forth from him. "I'm the one tied up, and you're seriously asking me to promise you safety?"

"You're a wolf."

"That I am, little doe."

"My mama told me about wolves."

"May I ask what she said?"

"The only good wolf was a dead one."

Hmm, seemed like he might have his work cut out for him trying to convince her otherwise. "And what do you think?"

"Actually, I was just wondering if what Grandma said was true."

"Which was?"

"That wolf pelts make warm winter coats."

"I'd have said we make better rugs."

"Really? Why?" More of her face came into view as she asked, her pert nose sprinkled with freckles, her pink lips pursed.

Tasty-looking. "There's nothing better than lying atop a wolf in front of a roaring fire. Your fingers gripping my pelt as your sweating body rides me to a howling, fun conclusion."

Those perfect lips rounded into an "O" of shock almost as big as her saucer-sized eyes. "You have a dirty mouth!"

"All the better to do dirty things with." He winked. His flirting didn't have the desired effect. Instead of smiling at him and coming closer, put at ease by his playful banter, the doe scampered off, a distant door slamming shut.

Damn. I think I might have come on too strong.

4

DAWN LEANED against the front door of the cabin, heart racing, blood heated, cheeks flushed and mind utterly shocked. It wasn't that she'd never been propositioned before. She had, and she wasn't a virgin, or a prude. Her time in the facility as a prisoner of the Mastermind meant she'd gotten more than her share of innuendos and offers, but crude attempts to get in her pants usually left her cold. Grossed out even.

I'm not that kind of girl. Her mother had raised her to have respect for herself and her body. It was why the two times she'd gone all the way with a boy, she'd made sure she felt something for them and them for her. They'd dated for a while before even reaching that stage.

So why was it the banged-up, obviously delirious wolf tied to her bed, wearing only a sheet, made her want to throw caution to the wind and see if he *would* make a comfortable rug?

Even his salacious wink, which should have made

her wrinkle her nose in disgust, had a most unexpected effect. Her lower regions tingled as she wondered if he could live up to the boast in his grin.

That man is dangerous. Not just because he was a predator, but also because he was obviously a rake such as she used to read about in her romance novels. Maybe he wasn't a lord or a pirate, but there was no denying, with those sideburns and sculpted body, he could play the part of dashing bad boy.

Which is so not my type. Especially since, given he was a FUC agent, he'd probably kill her in a second if he suspected who she was. Earlier she'd mistaken his uttered "fuck" for a curse, but now that she knew he was a shifter, it made more sense. It also was certainly no coincidence he'd ended up in these woods. Someone must have reported her, or one of the other experiments roaming these parts, to the agency. Her hiding place was compromised. She'd have to move on. Bummer.

First, though, she needed to go back inside, back to the wolf who was in the room where she kept her only knapsack and change of clothing. A part of her screamed "danger!" and advised her to walk away, or even better, run. Going back in for her meager belongings wasn't worth the risk. The wolf couldn't be trusted, even if he was currently trussed like a chicken.

However, she refused to start over again with only the clothes on her back. Bad enough she'd had to beg for money to buy food when she'd first escaped and stolen garments just so she wouldn't have to wander around naked. Paltry belongings or not, she would pack a bag and then head out.

What about the wolf, though?

She couldn't set him free. He'd be on her like a pig in a trough full of scraps. Yet, if she left him tied, how long before someone found him? By the look of things, the ramshackle cottage hadn't seen any summer visitors in a few seasons.

Gnawing on her lip, she marched back in and hoped for an answer. As it turned out, his first comment to her made it quite simple.

5

"Little doe, little doe, where are you?" he chanted as he heard a door open and her steps approaching.

"Right here. What do you want?"

You. That was his first thought when he'd seen her in all her plump, timid glory. Attempting to look tough, his petite captor and savior stood framed in the doorway, arms crossed under her boobs, expression set in a stern glare, which she couldn't hold as he laughed.

"What's so funny?"

"You. You do realize I've seen tougher looking chipmunks."

"I'm stronger than I look," she replied, her tone indignant.

He snickered as he said, "I'm sure you are."

"Don't make fun of me. I am not a weakling. Who do you think got you to this cabin, into this bed? By herself, I might add."

Huh. He'd not thought of that. His brow wrinkled as he tried to recall if he'd seen or scented anyone else since he regained consciousness. "No way. You must have had help."

She shook her head. "Nope. All me, so before you think I'm easy pickings, think again." Stalking over to the only dresser in the room, she tugged open drawers and began to stuff a knapsack she pulled from under the bed.

"Going somewhere?"

She didn't reply.

Someone was ticked. "Mind letting me go before you do?"

She snorted.

"Is that a no?"

Zipping her bag shut first, she took her time before turning and replying. "I'm not stupid enough to let a FUC agent, and a wolf, loose."

"I'm not a FUC agent."

"But you are a wolf."

"Can't deny that. It doesn't mean we can't be friends."

She snorted again. "Like that's going to happen." She tugged the straps of her knapsack over her arms.

"So you're just going to abandon me here?"

"I'm sure your friends will find you and free you, eventually."

His friend, as in Tom? If he waited for that sloth to arrive, he'd probably die of starvation. "It's just me, little doe."

"I'm sure the agency will come looking for you when you don't report in."

"I already told you, I don't work for FUC." Not anymore.

She paused in the doorway. "And I think you're lying. I heard you say their name when you first came to on the shore."

Stupid acronym. Only another shapeshifter would mistake fuck for FUC "I wasn't talking about the agency, but more the situation."

"Oh."

"So now will you let me go?"

She didn't hesitate this time. "No."

"Why not?"

"Because I don't trust you."

Smart girl. "What if I promise to leave you alone?"

"Red Riding Hood might have fallen for that line, but I've seen the movies and read the books. No. I am sorry. I'm usually a very nice person, but circumstances have made it so that I have to think of myself first. Good luck escaping. If I can, I'll send a ranger by to untie you."

If she could? Everett could only watch in disbelief as the doe actually left. Listened as the door to the place slammed shut. Then nothing.

She'd abandoned him.

Damn. He'd have to get himself free on his own. No way was he waiting for rescue, not if he wanted to retain his man card. As a wolf and a member of the male species, he couldn't have it bandied about that he was bested by a woman, and a woodland creature at that. His father would have a laughing fit and probably die of a coronary.

Nope. He needed to escape before anyone caught wind of his predicament. And when he caught up to her... He'd probably seduce her. Hey, it wasn't every day he came across a hottie with a bodacious butt like hers who turned him down. He loved a challenge. As for his mission? Perhaps he was mistaken about her being one of the fugitives on his list. No way was she one of those things he hunted. Speaking of which, he really should get moving. He wouldn't want his little doe to get caught by the murderous gecko. If anyone got to sink his teeth into that succulent flesh, it would be him.

Eyeing the rope that bound him, he quickly came to the conclusion that breaking it wasn't going to happen, nor could he reach the tough nylon to gnaw through the knots. The bed, on the other hand, had definitely seen better days. Despite his arms and legs being tied, he could bounce his ass. Up and down he thrust, the harsh squeak of tired springs loud.

Mental note to self. *If I do drag her back for seduction, skip the bed; too noisy and distracting.* Not to mention, he didn't think the bed would survive what he planned.

Bucking like a wild bronco on Viagra—minus the hard-on—Everett put the old-fashioned tarnished brass bed to work. It took a marathon session of cursing, hip thrusting, and yanking, but in the end, the bolts holding the headboard to the frame snapped. It didn't set him free immediately, but did allow him to bring his bound wrists to his mouth where his teeth made quick work of the knots. A few more minutes to take care of his ankles and he was free, naked as the day he was born, still banged up, but no longer a tempting YouTube video for Tom if he arrived—or a buffet for the monster if he located Everett first.

Bounding off the collapsed mattress, Everett winced

only a little as his still healing wounds reminded him of how he'd been snagged by the doe in the first place. She'd done a good job of cleaning him up, but in truth, he should thank his Lycan genes for the quick healing. Stretching out his cramped muscles, he took stock of his location as he stalked into the main area of the cabin. Rustic place with its plywood cupboards covered in tattered fabric, brown-stained sink, and mismatched plaid couch and chair. A great hiding spot for a fugitive, but not so great for a naked man in need of clothing.

It didn't take him long to decide he needed to go after the doe as a wolf. If humans saw his shaggy beast, he'd attract attention, but not as much as a streaking male would. He shifted and, immediately, his senses sharpened. Smells became more distinct, his eyesight caught even the minutest details, and the chill on his flesh disappeared as his thick fur kept him warm.

On four paws, he entered the dense forest. The female might have gotten a head start, but her trail was simple to follow, until she hit the creek.

He lost her scent at that point, not for lack of trying. Up and down the minor riverbed he traveled, nose in the air, trying to sniff where she'd emerged from the gurgling stream. But it was if she'd vanished into thin air. He located many tracks—skunk, raccoon, squirrel, moose even, but no doe.

Darn it. She'd escaped.

With night falling and Tom surely freaking, and, don't forget, a monster on the loose, Everett had to call the search off. He wasn't quitting, though. Not by a long shot. The little doe needed to be found and not just because of the bounty on her cute head.

No one messes with the big, bad wolf. Time someone taught an impertinent doe that lesson.

It took him the rest of the afternoon to make his way back to the parking lot where he'd left the SUV parked. He arrived limping, tired, cranky, and hungry, which made the sight of Tom, sitting in the passenger seat snoozing, all the more irritating.

He banged on the window on his way to the trunk. Opening the back, he snagged some of the clothes he kept in a gym bag.

"About time you came back. The cooler's empty and I was getting hungry." Tom craned in his seat and cracked a huge yawn.

"Thanks for your concern."

Tom raised a bushy brow. "You were only gone just over sixteen hours. Not unusual for you when you're on the trail of something. What happened to 'don't get worried unless it's been a week?'"

Everett grimaced. "That was before I ran into a ginormous mutant lizard who almost crushed me to death before dropping me off a cliff and then got captured by a deer who tied me to a bed."

Tom ogled Everett. "What?"

Ignoring his query, Everett scrounged around in their truck for something to gnaw on. Not finding a T-bone steak, he settled for a stale granola bar he found squished in the glove compartment.

"What happened out there?"

"Oh-ho. So now he wants to know. Where should I start? With the monster who, by the laws of science, shouldn't exist?"

"As if. Start with the girl. The one who tied you to a

bed. What did she want? She didn't, you know, *force* you, did she?" Tom's question sounded half hopeful, half jealous.

I wish. "Get your dirty mind out of the gutter. She tied me up as a safety precaution. Apparently, she worried I might eat her."

"Oh, so it was a human then who caught you while in wolf form."

"No. She was a shifter, and I was in my man shape when I came to, naked and tied to a bed."

Tom practically drooled. "So, what did she want you for?"

He shrugged. "Nothing. She found me half dead on the side of the river and somehow managed to get me back to some abandoned cabin where she cleaned me up before abandoning me." He couldn't help a note of disgruntlement. It still irked him she'd just gone and left him there.

A choked snort escaped Tom then a full-out belly laugh. "Oh my God. You're peeved because she didn't fall for your charm. That's priceless. And probably a first."

"Not every woman falls under my spell." Married ones, some of them at least, tended to have immunity.

"I wish I could have met her," Tom said, still chuckling. "But back to the first part of your trek. You say you found the mutant lizard? Did you kill it?"

"No. Damned thing nearly killed me. And it wasn't just any lizard, but the gecko on the list of creatures FUC wants us to find. The thing's a freaking monster, though. I'm going to need a gun, a big one, before we go after it again." Maybe even a flame thrower. Or, like a dragon, would its skin prove impervious to flame? At this point, nothing would surprise him.

"Want to call in some backup?"

And admit he'd run into something he couldn't handle? He scratched his balls, reasserting his masculinity. "No. I won't need it because I am not chasing the lizard."

"What do you mean? We can't just let it roam around."

"I know. I know. But first we've got to find someone else."

Tom caught on quickly. "Not the girl? Let her be. She didn't want you. It's not the end of the world."

"One, I am going after her for her own good. It's not safe in the park right now. And two, if I'm not mistaken, she's also on the list of fugitives FUC wants back. She needs to be caught." And, no, this wasn't about his wounded male pride. Okay, maybe just a little.

6

DAWN WADED UP THE CREEK, without a paddle or a boat, not too far, though. While the water would mask her trail, it also slowed her down and, right now, speed was of the essence, but so was covering her tracks. When she did step forth from the bubbling brook, she had her Ziploc bag with its pre-scented booties ready.

From a young age, those on the low end of the food chain—in other words, deer, which were considered a yummy delicacy by carnivores—learned how to protect themselves. Odor was the biggest issue. As her dad had explained to her during one of his rare moments of parenting, if a predator got her scent, short of shooting it dead, once they got on her tail, she was no better than buttered toast. Or as Grandma used to say, "You're more screwed than a bunny in heat."

Thankfully, as a shifter, she possessed more brains than a simple doe. No staring into approaching headlights for her or, in this case, waiting for a wolf's bite. Her daddy taught her well—and her grandma even better. Right after her escape from the FUC facility, she'd not just clothed herself before hitting the woods. She'd also grabbed some airtight sandwich bags, some fabric booties, and the strongest raccoon pee the local outdoor store sold. A spritz of it on her body and a soaking of the slippers, which she pulled over her feet, meant when she left the cleansing water of the creek, she left behind a scent trail, just not her own.

Follow that, Mr. Wolf. She didn't doubt for an instant the virile male she'd left behind would escape his bonds, and when he did, he'd probably come looking for her. Wounded pride would force him. Also, despite his claim he didn't work for FUC, she couldn't help but wonder what he was doing in those woods. Coincidence or not? She'd never found out how he got injured, but judging by the bruises and contusions before they'd healed, she'd guess he'd battled something big. Given these forests weren't known for rampaging bears or wildcats, she could only assume he'd run into the psycho gecko whose trail she'd crossed a few times in her ramblings.

Thus far, the creature, an experiment just like her, had left her alone. Solidarity perhaps because of their past history as prisoners? Or something more... Joey always did show more of an interest in her than she liked, both behind bars and when in the supposed FUC safe house.

She suspected a crush, which, while not returned, might just protect her stubby tail from the gecko's wrath. However, she doubted the wolf's tango with the giant lizard would go unreported. The wolf was sure to call in its presence once he achieved freedom and found a phone, which meant her hiding spot was compromised.

Time to find a new place to go, but here was where she ran into a problem.

Hundreds of miles of protected forest land meant great hiding, but, with no supplies, she'd soon starve. Not to mention, she needed shelter. Fall was waning, which meant winter approached with icy footsteps. Foraging in human or deer form wouldn't be possible for much longer. She needed to get out of these woods and find somewhere to hunker down.

She didn't dare exit from the main entrance to the national park. Chances were good Mr. Wolf waited for her there. However, there was more than one way out of the forest. Hitching her bag higher up on her back, she set off west, knowing it would take at least a day, maybe more, for her to traverse the miles between her and the hamlet bordering the one-lane highway leading to nowhere.

Seriously. The places the government put roads sometimes. It boggled the mind, but suited her purposes. The farther from civilization she got, the less chance she'd run into someone working for FUC—and shifters who might recognize she wasn't quite all she appeared.

So it was, more than forty-three hours later, grimy, tired, hungry, and with sore feet, that she emerged from the forest. Not quite where she hoped. The town remained a mile or so north of her, but the tarmac proved a welcome change to her stumbling feet. At least now she didn't have to contend with hidden roots tangling her up, branches slapping her in the face, and the sensation that something watched.

It had occurred to her more than once to change shapes, her doe more surefooted for this kind of terrain, but the occasional shots of poachers, their gunfire echoing all around, was a grim reminder that not all dangers came on four legs. As she had little desire to end up on the mantel of some eager hunter, she put on her brightest top and stayed a human.

The wee town, when she trudged in to it, was barely existent. One tiny grocery store, a post office, hardware slash clothing boutique, and a greasy spoon. Her tummy rumbled as the welcome scent of home-cooked fries, bacon, and ground beef wafted out to her. Ever since her change, she'd migrated from her lifelong vegetarian diet to one that now included meat. Cooked meat, thank goodness, but still. She tried not to think of how the animals got onto her plate, but couldn't stop the saliva from pooling in her mouth at the thought of sinking her teeth into a juicy beef burger—pink on the inside.

With just over forty dollars to her name, she needed to make a choice. While the greasy spoon would fulfill her immediate hunger pangs, it would deplete her reserves. She sighed. Much as it sucked, she opted for the grocery store where she could make her dollar stretch further.

She didn't quite make it. From behind, an arm snaked around her waist, and a gruff, yet velvety, voice murmured in her ear, "By all the unshaven hairs on my chinny, chin, chin, look at what I found. Hello, little doe. Happy to see me?"

7

Everett expected a scream. Maybe a bit of a struggle. He even tensed his abs for an elbow. What he didn't expect was wry laughter.

"If it isn't the big, bad wolf. I should have known better than to tempt fate and wear my red hoodie."

He grimaced. "Talk about being cliché."

Again, her laughter rang out, an all-too-pleasant sound. "Not intentionally. When trekking through the woods during hunting season, it's always best to make sure you're not mistaken for something else."

"So long as we're not reliving that annoying tale." While Everett did enjoy quoting some of the more famous lines in the wolf tales, he always hated how, in the end, the wolf always got screwed. And not in a good way.

"Oh, I don't know, didn't the girl prevail in the end over the wolf? Seems to me, I like the way that story went."

"I prefer the more modern version," he said as he

turned her in his grasp so she faced him. Her slight figure fit perfectly against him, a fact a certain part of his anatomy couldn't help but notice.

She didn't struggle, which he took as a good sign. She peered at his face as she asked, "Which modern version?"

"The X-rated one where the girl in the red hood exclaims over what a big—"

His little doe slapped her hand over his mouth before he could say it. It didn't stop his grin, though. "Don't you dare," she threatened.

"Prude," he mumbled against the palm of her hand. He couldn't resist the temptation and gave her a lick.

A frown creased her face as she yanked her hand away and rubbed it against her pant leg, a not so subtle rebuke at his attempt to seduce. She angled her chin and threw him a haughty glance. "I prefer the term lady."

"I'd rather call you by your real name. I'm Everett. Everett Johnson."

He couldn't help a growing interest south of his belt buckle when her pearly white teeth gnawed at her lower lip as she debated what to tell him. Would she lie and tell him her name was Bambi? She didn't look like any Bambi he'd ever encountered, and he'd met quite a few during his support of local bars and their amateur dancers. Before judging, keep in mind the dollars he'd spent at the clothing optional locales helped many a young lady pay for college. Just doing his part to support education.

"Come on, don't be shy. You've already seen my

impressive man bits, the least you can do is tell me your name."

"Impressive according to who?"

He took in a big breath, ready to get indignant, when he caught the slight curl of her lip. The minx. She goaded him. Ha. He was more than a match for her teasing. "Huff and puff on it and I'll show you." He couldn't help tossing her a wink and a wide grin.

How awesome the way she managed to redden brighter than her sweater. "I can't believe you said that."

"I can't believe you blushed. Didn't that kind of modesty go out with ankle-length skirts?"

"Someone needs to wash your mouth out with soap."

"My mother tried that."

"And?"

"She didn't find the bubble I blew out my nose very entertaining. But we weren't discussing how I became so awesome. You were about to give me your name."

"No I wasn't."

"I'll pants you in public if you don't." Ah, how cute. There she went turning red again.

"That is the most juvenile threat I've ever heard."

"Yup, and yet, I'll do it. Hope you shaved your girl parts, or we might hear some screams of 'Sasquatch.'"

She sighed and shook her head. "I knew I should have used handcuffs."

"Mmm, kinky. If you want, we can go back to the cabin so you can try again."

With a roll of her eyes, she muttered. "You wish, wolf."

"The name, as I mentioned before, is Everett, and you are..." He peered at her expectantly.

She sighed. "Dawn."

"Dawn who?"

"Doesn't matter."

"Well, Dawn Doesn't-Matter, can I buy you a piece of pie?"

"I'd rather have a cheeseburger and some fries," she said wistfully.

"Deal." Because, as it so happened, he could use a bite to eat too.

"Wait a second, deal for what?"

"I buy you all you can eat, and you tell me why FUC wants you back, dead or alive."

"Dead!" She squeaked. "But I didn't do anything."

"Not going to deny you're on their list of escapees?"

Her shoulders slumped. "Is there any point?"

"No."

"Then I won't deny it."

"Come on, we'll talk it over with some food." Because there was no mistaking the grumble of her tummy. Dangerous fugitive or not, if he had to guess, he'd wager Dawn had missed one too many meals.

They seated themselves in the corner of the restaurant at opposite ends of a worn leather booth, the cushions bandaged with duct tape. He waited for the waitress to dump a pair of plastic-coated menus before bombarding her with questions.

"So, Dawn, what's the scoop? Why are you considered a menace to society?"

Her nose scrunched. "I'd hardly call myself a menace."

"Says the girl who left me tied to a bed."

"Oh, please. I'm sure it's not the first time." Her sly innuendo had her ducking her head, but she couldn't hide her smirk. Shy, demure, with a touch of mischievous. He was liking her more and more.

"No, not the first time, but usually the lady in question sticks around to enjoy her handiwork."

The comment made her squirm in her seat. "I'm not that kind of girl."

"A shame." Really, it was. "But enough teasing, and avoiding the question. Why is it you're wanted? Are you a traitor to shifter kind? A spy? A serial killer masquerading as a cute and harmless woodland creature?"

"How about none of the above?"

"There's got to be a reason they're offering such a substantial reward for your return."

"Ever gotten screwed for being in the wrong place at the right time?"

More like the right place at the right time, but he nodded so she'd continue.

"They want me because of an accident. A few months ago, some hyena and a rat snagged me as I was coming home from work. Knocked me out cold. When I woke, I was in some cage, prisoner of someone called Mastermind."

"The rodent who wanted to rule the world?"

"Yes. That's her. The crazy critter kidnapped a bunch of us. I was lucky. The FUC crew arrived to the rescue only a few weeks into my incarceration, just before they were about to start me on some experimental drugs."

"What were they doing prior to that?"

"Analyzing me. They ran a gamut of tests on me—blood, exercise, stress, and more, so they could know everything about me before they started the trial drug runs. They wanted 'before' results so they could compare them to the 'after' ones. But after never came. Not at the institution where I was held prisoner at any rate."

"So you lucked out. Why weren't you released when FUC raided and saved you all?"

"I was injured during the attack. Nothing huge. A stray bullet caught me in the temple. She brushed back her hair and showed him a scarred, white furrow. "It caused temporary amnesia so they kept me in a secure location to treat me with the other rescued prisoners. I remembered who I was just before the fateful night when Mastermind injected us all with a chemical cocktail."

"Bummer."

"Big bummer. A lot of the patients went crazy that night from the drug. They killed the nurses and guards. Went on a wild rampage. During the chaos, I escaped."

"Did you go wild too?"

"A little, but not murderously so. I just knew I had to get out of there. To escape. My animal took over, and I blacked out for a while."

"What about when you came to your senses? Why didn't you return?"

She slumped on her elbows. "I thought about it, but then it occurred to me, why should I? It was because of FUC I'd ended up worse off than before. If they'd caught on to Mastermind even just a day before, I wouldn't have gotten injected and…"

"And what?"

"I'd rather not talk about it."

Their waitress returned, notepad in hand. They placed their order but remained silent because their server returned immediately with their drinks—coffee for him, a giant vanilla milkshake for her.

He went at her from a different angle. "You aren't the only fugitive in the woods. I came across something else, some kind of lizard."

"You mean Joey?"

"I don't know who or what the hell he is other than nasty, about eight feet tall, and very freaking hungry."

"Sounds like Joey. He started out as a gecko and used to be an all right sort of fellow, I guess. He lived in a jail cell a few up from me. As far as I recall, he was pretty quiet, a docile type of guy who wouldn't even eat a fly. At least the old Joey wouldn't. But that's what the injection did to him. The drug, on top of everything else Joey suffered at Mastermind's hand, turned him into a science project gone horribly wrong."

"So you've seen him?"

"Glimpses. Mostly I avoided him. Joey knew I was in the woods, but left me alone. I take it you didn't enjoy the same luck?"

"Nope. It's how I ended up on the shore of that river where you found me."

"And should have left you," she grumbled under her breath before sucking on the straw of her milkshake. Pursed lips, cheeks hollowed, she brought to mind something he really shouldn't be thinking of in a public restaurant. Thank the full moon the table hid his inevitable boner.

"If the cocktail mutated this harmless Joey fellow into a monster, what did it do to you? You said it changed you, and yet you seem perfectly normal."

"I am. More or less. It's my deer side that's changed."

"Enough that FUC thinks you're a threat to society."

"I'm not a danger."

"So you claim."

"So I know."

"Then why won't you tell me what it did to you?"

"Because."

"Because why?" he pressed.

She growled.

Her. A doe. Growling at him, a wolf. Seriously? "What the hell was that?"

"Please stop. You're aggravating my animal."

Aggravating a deer to the point she threatened him? He almost laughed, but given the expression on her face—part frightened, part crazy—he held off for now. "All right, little doe, but this isn't over." Not by a long shot. Far from convincing him to back down with her threat, now, more than ever, he wanted to know what she hid.

The waitress arrived with two plates heaped high. He'd gone for a chicken club sandwich with fries and onion rings while Dawn got the half-pound burger, medium rare, garnished with the works, accompanied by fries, onion rings, and gravy. Forget the stereotypical woman, or doe, eating a light salad. There was enough grease on her plate to stop a heart in its tracks.

As she inhaled her steaming food—good grief the

woman could eat!—his cell phone vibrated in his jeans pocket. Everett dug it out and checked the display before answering. "Hey, Tom."

"I'm bored. Are we done watching for the deer yet? I'm tired of sitting in my car when I've got a perfectly good bed calling my name at home. You lost her, dude. Get over it."

Eyeing the *her* in question, Everett debated how to reply. "You're right. It's a lost cause. Why don't you head back to your place? I'm just going to grab some dinner then I'll be hitting the hay as well. We'll regroup in the morning."

A groan came through his phone's speaker. "Not more deer watching?"

"Nope. I'm done looking for her. It's time we planned our attack on the monster."

"Me and my big mouth," Tom grumbled. "Fine. But, just so you know, I think we should have stuck to human bail jumpers. It's safer."

Safer, easier, and boring. Tom could complain all he wanted, but he'd help hunt the monster because the sloth possessed a strong sense of civic duty. To shifters at least.

Everett hung up and tucked his phone away. When his gaze strayed to Dawn, he found her staring at him.

"Why didn't you tell your friend you found me?"

Good question, one he didn't have a clear answer to. He shrugged. "He didn't need to know."

She nibbled on a fry, again conjuring an image of what else she could nibble on. At this rate, he'd need an ice pack to settle his dick down.

"What are you? You said before you weren't a FUC

agent, but you weren't in that forest by chance, and you're pretty well informed for a civilian, even a shifter one."

"I'm a fugitive recovery agent."

She stared at him blankly.

"I catch escaped criminals and collect the bounties on them when I bring them back to the proper authorities."

"Oh. So that's why you were in the woods. You were looking to capture me and make some money."

"You, the gecko, and any other shifters on the FUC wanted list." No point in lying.

"How much are they offering for me?"

"A decent chunk, but I'm not planning on collecting it." Whoa. Wait a second. Since when? He hated it when his mind made decisions for him without letting him know first.

She seemed equally surprised. "You're not?"

"Not yet at any rate. But don't think this means I'm letting you go free. I might not be working for FUC, but that doesn't mean I'm just going to let you run loose, not without making sure you're not dangerous first."

"And how do you plan to do that?"

He couldn't help a toothy grin. "You and I are about to become close friends." Joined at the hip or, if lucky, much more *interesting* places.

Her slim brows drew together. "I'm afraid I still don't understand."

"You, my little doe, will be coming home with me."

8

If I end up as dinner, I'll only have myself to blame.

Dawn peered around the obviously masculine living room and wondered once again how he'd convinced her to come here, smack dab in the wolf's lair. *Have I completely lost my mind?*

When Everett had initially told her he intended to bring her to his home, she'd laughed, so hard she practically fell off her chair, only to realize he was quite serious. What surprised her more than his intention was how easily she'd acquiesced. Belly full, more relaxed than she'd felt in weeks, and, oddly enough, entertained by the attractive male, she found herself agreeing, with a few conditions.

One, she got her own bed, in this case his bed, since he only owned one. He'd sleep on the couch. Two, he was to tell no one of her presence. Three, once she proved she was harmless, he'd let her go. Where, she still had no idea, but so long as it didn't involve a jail cell, or more doctors, she was pretty easy. Just not the kind of easy he hoped for.

"Welcome to the Wolf's Den," Everett announced from behind her.

"More like the three pigs' sty." She wrinkled her nose as she turned to face him. "When was the last time you tidied the place or thought to use a vacuum?"

"I've been busy."

Bending down, she snagged a pizza box with a receipt taped to the top. "This was bought almost four months ago."

A red flush inched its way to his cheeks. "So the place could use a little help."

"Little? Try a lot. You've got some fuzzy stuff in here that's about ready to splinter off and start a colony."

"Excuse me for lacking housekeeping skills," he snapped defensively.

"Then hire someone."

"I haven't had the time."

But she did, for the moment. "I've got a deal for you. Since I'm going to need some money for when I leave, how about I clean the place for you in exchange for a paycheck?"

"Isn't keeping you safe, feeding you, and giving you the pleasure of my company enough?"

She snorted. "No." She waved a hand around. "Considering I'm exposing myself to all kinds of probably toxic substances and possible mutant life, I'd say you're getting off cheap."

"Fine. I'll pay you. I never knew deer were so stubborn."

"My great grandfather was a mule."

The bark of laughter and subsequent smile on Everett's face just about stopped her heart. Gosh, he was cute. Hair sticking out in all directions or not, scruffy beard on his chin, sideburns that should have looked dumb but didn't. Wearing disreputable clothes that had probably never seen better days, he was everything she usually avoided in a man. Yet, she couldn't deny his appeal.

Unlike her preppy ex-boyfriends, always perfectly well behaved and dressed, Everett was a wild one. He didn't temper his comments, didn't give a damn about appearances, and didn't treat her like a delicate princess. It was refreshing, attractive, and confusing. Given the turmoil in her life right now, the last thing she needed was to form an attachment, even one she didn't intend to pursue, especially for a male who admitted he'd initially planned to turn her in for money. As for his current intentions… The hunger in his eyes plainly said he wouldn't mind taking a bite out of her, an erotic bite. Eep!

He gave her the grand tour of his small bungalow, each room just as messy as the living room. The kitchen was a write-off. No way was she eating anything in there until it got a Lysol bomb. The most surprisingly clean location was his bathroom. She could actually see the floor in there. As for his bedroom…

"Welcome to the love cave," he purred as he swept out an arm and gestured her in.

"Ugh. Please don't tell me that line actually works?" Hard to believe with the piles of laundry heaped all over.

"Actually, I'm more of a sleep-over type of guy."

"Of course you are. It's much easier to ignore a woman the next day if she doesn't know where you live."

He clutched his chest and staggered. "Ouch! That was cruel, little doe."

"Sorry." Not. He was a womanizer and made no bones about it.

"I know how you can make it better." He waggled his brows.

She pursed her lips. "By making sure you don't need a tetanus shot. This place is a biohazard. I might have to ask for a supplement on my paycheck given the danger."

He growled. "I am really beginning to question my decision to bring you here instead of straight to the FUC lockup."

"A deal's a deal."

"Lucky for you, I'm a wolf of my word."

Lucky indeed. Dawn knew she should stop baiting Everett. He was, after all, keeping to his side of the bargain so far by not turning her in. But teasing him came so easily, and she got the impression he didn't actually mind it. As she gingerly stepped around the strewn clothing, putting some space between her and the wolf, she asked, "Do you have any clean sheets?"

"Maybe. Somewhere." For some reason, her request seemed to fluster him. "Listen, I've got to go out for a little while. Will you be all right if I leave you alone?"

She couldn't help arching a brow. "I don't need a babysitter."

"I wasn't implying you did. I was more wondering

if I can trust you to stay here and not run. Or do I need to take you with me?"

"Are you doubting my word?"

"Little doe, in my line of work, you doubt everyone."

Fair enough. "I promised you I'd stay until I could prove myself safe to shifters and humans. I am a woman of my word."

"I hope so. I'll be back in a bit. Make yourself at home."

If she were at home, she'd have a clean spot to sit. And sleep. If she thought the living room was messy, his room appeared as if a tornado had gone through.

First things first, if she intended to sleep in the bed, the sheets had to go, as did the many piles of clothes, which she didn't bother checking for cleanliness. She assumed they were all dirty and took armfuls to the hall where the washer and dryer hid in a closet. She got a large load going then went hunting for cleaning supplies.

By some stroke of luck, she found a clean set of sheets, still in packaging, in the almost empty linen closet. With the hour approaching midnight and her eyes drooping from fatigue, she quickly made the bed and collapsed in it. Messy house or not, the wolf owned a comfortable mattress, and she fell into an immediate sleep, one rudely interrupted hours later by a very drunk, naked wolf, who crawled into bed and sprawled across it, a heavy leg and arm flung over her.

"Get off me," she squeaked, pushing at him. Her hands encountered male flesh wherever she touched. Hot, very nude, and oh so tempting male flesh.

One bleary eye opened and peered at her. "Hey, little doe."

"Don't you hey me. What are you doing?"

"Trying to sleep."

"In my bed."

"Don't you mean my bed?"

"Which you said I could have."

"I did?"

"You did."

"Okay." He closed his eye and didn't budge.

"Um, Everett. You need to move."

"But it's my bed."

"And I'm in it."

"Yes, and I have to say that was a pleasant surprise." His hand, which rested on her tummy, inched along her ribcage until it cupped a breast. She squirmed to no avail as he brushed a finger over her nipple, which, despite the fabric covering it, perked into a taut peak. As for her girly parts further south? They stirred with interest. She clamped her thighs tight.

This wouldn't do at all. She tried again. "Everett, wake up. You need to move."

He nuzzled her instead as he grumbled a bleary, "Why?"

She fought the shiver at his touch and lifted her head out of his reach. "Because you're supposed to sleep on the couch. Remember?"

"But it's lumpy." He opened his eyes and his lower lip jutted into a pout. "Can't we share?"

Share the bed with a naked, virile wolf who made her body hum with a desire she could ill afford to indulge in?

"No, we can't share." Her protest fell on deaf ears as Everett closed his eyes again and snored, not softly either.

Darn it. Now what was she supposed to do? The only option left to her, given he kept her caged with an arm and a leg. Sleep—and dream. Dream naughty things where a predator ate his prey, to her blissful delight.

9

Waking with a woman atop him wasn't new to Everett. Discovering the woman in question was Dawn made his eyes shoot open. *Uh-oh.* How had he ended up wearing her as a blanket in his bed?

His recollection of the previous night was fuzzy at best. Ridiculous amounts of alcohol would do that even to a shifter who could metabolize it faster than a human. In his defense, he'd needed the booze so he could try and forget the doe. Something about her delicate nature, which covered a firm backbone—ending in a sexy tail—drew this lone wolf. Drew and attracted him to the point he couldn't stop thinking about her.

What was a wolf to do? Seduce her? A usual course of action if he'd not kind of told her he'd give her his bed, without him in it. Stupid honor thing. Why couldn't he be more like his brothers and break promises faster than he could make them? But Everett, despite his bad-boy image, had morals. If he promised something, he stuck to it, even if it hurt. And, boy, did his promise to leave Dawn alone hurt his poor, raging libido. Worried he'd do something to ruin her timidly given trust—say like drag her into his arms and kiss her breathless—he'd needed to escape.

With a doe on his brain, instead of on his cock, and in need of distraction, he resorted to what many a man did in this situation. He got drunk to forget. He'd done so well he'd forgotten he'd promised her his bed. What surprised him was she hadn't kicked him out of it.

What else don't I remember?

Given he found himself naked, and she remained very much clothed, he doubted he'd gotten any nookie, but then again, with her sprawled atop him, trusting and intimate, perhaps he'd forgotten more than just how he got home after the bar closed.

It pleased him to note his trust in her wasn't misplaced. He'd wondered at first, as he sat in his truck just up the street with a dozen beers he'd snagged from his fridge before leaving, if she'd flee at the first chance. But no. He'd watched her silhouette in the curtained windows as she moved in and out of his bedroom, making several trips, more than likely trying to create a path through the chaos. When the light eventually flicked off, he'd left his truck and crept close for a peek. A gap in the fabric covering his window and the streetlight let him observe her sleeping, peaceful as an angel, hair spread across the pillow, face relaxed, fingers clutching at the sheet—*in my bed, where she belongs*. It took more willpower than he liked not to crawl in alongside her.

Disturbed at the thought, he'd left and gone to his local bar, where he drank. And drank some more until everything faded away, even his need for the doe. He'd forgotten so well he'd ended up in the one place he was trying to avoid—and hornier than an unneutered, three-balled lupine.

Any chance she'd not noticed him crawling into bed last night? Not likely.

Was there any way to extricate himself without waking her? Nope.

And why was he acting like some emasculated excuse of a male?

Grabbing her ass cheeks with two hands and the lobe of her ear with his teeth, in a gruff morning voice, he murmured, "By all the hair on my impressive chest, good morning, little doe. Fancy finding you here."

The scream he understood, the thrashing as well, but the knee to his groin as she scrambled to get away from him and the gagging? Totally uncalled for.

"Eew!" She fanned her face. "Did something crawl in your mouth and die?"

Well, that shriveled his happy morning erection quicker than a cold shower. "Excuse me for not brushing my teeth yet. Kind of hard with a forest animal using me as a pillow."

Aw, how cute. She blushed. He still didn't forgive her for the throbbing in his groin. Not until she offered to kiss it better.

Alas, a kiss for his booboo wasn't on the agenda.

She went on the attack. "You broke your promise. You said I could have the bed."

"And you did."

"Alone."

"I forgot."

"Because you were drunk," she accused, shaking her finger. Talk about an inappropriate time to want to suck on that digit. "I reminded you last night, but you refused to leave."

Oops. He didn't remember that part. "I don't suppose I can say I'm sorry?"

She tossed her hair. "Apology accepted, if you go to Starbucks."

"What?" Her quick forgiveness followed by her imperious demand made his already spinning head wobble on his shoulders, much like the yellow bobble-head minion on the dash of his truck.

"I said, if you want me to accept your apology, then I want Starbucks. There is nothing edible in this house."

She had a point. Still… "Do you know how much they charge for coffee?"

"About as much as they do for one of their breakfast wraps. And I want two. Also, a blueberry scone and a cinnamon bun. Oh, and I like my coffee large, extra sugar, triple cream with a shot of caramel."

Docile? How had he ever thought that? "Anything else, princess?"

She smiled, and it was brighter than the eye-squinting morning sunlight streaming through his window—and utterly captivating. "As a matter of fact, yes."

"I'm almost afraid to ask what."

"I made a list last night. Just a few essentials if I'm going to stay here." She grabbed a sheet from his cleared nightstand and handed it to him.

Everett perused it, his brows getting higher and

higher the more he read. "Tampons! You expect me to go shopping for tampons?"

"And pads. I'm going to need both to prevent spillage."

Too much information. Especially this early in the morning. "No way." He thrust the list back at her.

She crossed her arms and refused to take it. "I need those things. You promised to take care of me while I was your guest. Are you breaking your word, again?" A pointed stare at the bed had him gnashing his teeth.

"How about I just give you money and you go shopping for these items yourself?"

"While I appreciate your trust, how am I supposed to do that on foot?"

"I'll loan you my truck." As soon as the words came out of his mouth, he clamped his lips tight. Was he a complete idiot? Offering to give her money and wheels? Hello, she'd just neatly maneuvered him into giving her the perfect escape.

To his surprise, she didn't jump on his offer. "I don't want your truck. I can't drive."

"You can't drive?" He ogled her. "Seriously? What are you, like twenty-two, twenty-three?"

"Twenty-four actually, and no, I don't drive. I freeze in headlights." Her slim shoulders lifted, and she tossed him a wry smile. "I guess some things are just inherent."

For some reason, Everett found this immensely funny, and he chuckled and chuckled some more until someone hit him in the face with a clean pair of pants. How novel. He thought he'd run out last week and had planned on hitting Walmart for a new pair.

"Put those on."

"Why? I'm not cold."

"You are naked, though."

"Yup. And thank you for noticing." His dick waved hello, but she missed it, her gaze kept strictly on his face.

"I'd give you some underpants too, but I didn't find those when I did some laundry last night."

"That's 'cause I don't own any. I like to go commando."

Most women would blush or giggle at this admission. Dawn just made a face. "Gross."

"I prefer the term dangerous."

"And how is that?"

"Zippers aren't man's best friend."

It took her a moment to grasp his meaning, and when she did, her gaze flicked down. His dick pointed up, her cheeks flushed bright red, and she ran faster than a rabbit in front of a hungry wolf.

He almost chased her down because, as a red-blooded male, the view of that pert ass wiggling out of sight was a hard temptation to resist. But a promise was a promise. On went the pants. And, as if karma were waiting in the corner to bite him…his zipper caught a few hairs.

Awoo-ouch! His howl of shock almost drowned out her laughter.

10

Dawn fled to the kitchen, where the cupboards were bare, just like a certain man. It mortified her to no end that she'd woken atop Everett, a blanket for his nakedness. It shocked her even worse to realize she'd quite enjoyed it, until she'd caught a whiff of his beer-laden breath. It, and the position she found herself in, aided her in dispelling the extremely naughty thoughts of what she could do with all that tempting male flesh.

And, boy, did he have a lot of that. Apparently, it didn't matter she'd seen it before when she'd cared for him at the cabin. It still hit her like a ton of erotic bricks, right between the legs. Predator or not, she wanted to jump on his bone and gnaw until he howled. *He'd probably let me too. Even encourage it.* Everett didn't disguise the fact he wanted to have sex with her.

But I'm not that type of girl. Even if she wished otherwise at the moment.

The wolf in question sauntered into the kitchen, upper torso unclad and jeans hanging indecently low on his hips. With his jaw unshaven and sporting a few days' worth of stubble, he presented a delicious visual treat. Her pussy rumbled, kind of like her tummy. Two hungers, and he was the linchpin to solving them both.

"Are you going out like that?" she asked, keeping his small island between them as he paced the kitchen, his presence dwarfing the space.

"You forgot to give me a shirt."

So she had. "There's some on top of the dryer." She moved left, as he came at her from the right.

"Are you sure you wouldn't prefer to *eat* here?" There was nothing subtle about his hint, not given the way he said it and the smoldering glance he aimed her way.

She pretended to misunderstand, and ignored her treacherous body, which wanted to know why they couldn't take him up on his offer. "Eat what? The science experiment in the fridge?"

"Damn. Has the food already gone bad? I went shopping the first of the month."

"And it's now almost the end of it."

"Oh." His sheepish grin was adorable.

"How do you not starve?"

He shrugged as he leaned against the counter. "Restaurants are always happy to feed me, as are some of my friends."

Lady friends she'd bet with not a little twinge of jealousy. "Well, since you're such a connoisseur of the local eateries, mind grabbing a shirt and taking me to one? I'm starving." And not just for food.

"What happened to your Starbucks demand?"

"I changed my mind. I need something with a little more substance."

"I know where you can get some good morning sausage." He waggled his brows.

She burst out laughing. "That is so not attractive."

"Aren't you the slightest bit tempted?"

Yes, but her mother hadn't raised her to give in to temptation. And Grandma had taught her how to resist it—*"If you ever find yourself tempted by the wrong type of man, picture your daddy in his skimpy Speedos."* Shudder. "Sorry, but seeing your hairy caterpillar wiggle just makes me think of baby birds feeding."

Offended, he stalked off, and when he returned, not only did he wear a shirt and socks, but he'd shaved—chin, cheeks, and the spot between his eyebrows.

She bit her lip lest she giggle.

He took her to a local joint, which fed her eggs, bacon, ham, sausage, toast, and freshly squeezed orange juice. She also got a Danish for dessert. He then drove her over to a food mart where she stocked up on things, including her personal hygiene items, which made him grumble under his breath as he pushed the laden cart. They then returned to his home where a strange car sat parked in his driveway.

"Shit. I forgot about Tom."

"Who's Tom?" she asked as she hopped out of Everett's truck.

"He is." The *he* in question was a short but wide man, probably in his late thirties, early forties. Framed in the doorway of Everett's house, he raised a bushy brow in their direction.

Dawn's first instinct was to bolt, and as if sensing it,

Everett clamped a hand on her arm, just above her elbow and murmured, "It's all right. He won't hurt you."

She wasn't worried about him hurting her so much as she was afraid he'd turn her in.

"Everett." Tom drew out the name. "Please don't tell me that's who I think it is."

"Okay. I won't."

"I thought you didn't find her."

"No. You assumed I didn't. I just never bothered to correct you."

Crossing his arms over his barrel chest, his supposed friend glared. "Why is she here instead of in FUC custody?"

"*She* is standing right here and would prefer not to be spoken of in the third person." Drawing her spine straight to stare down the other man went against her usual docile nature, but Dawn's recently evolving more savage side enjoyed the match of wills.

Something in her gaze must have unnerved him because Tom raised his hands in a conciliatory gesture. "No offense meant, ma'am. I was just taken by surprise."

"Fair enough." Tom blinked first, breaking the match—*I won!*—but she highly doubted their minor altercation was over. She'd have to watch her step around the man. He seemed a tad too eager to sic FUC on her.

"Give me a hand bringing in the groceries." Everett let her go, apparently satisfied she wouldn't bolt. Brave of him considering she'd still not made up her mind. While the men loaded themselves with bags, she watched them warily while also keeping an eye on the street. Suddenly, she didn't trust the situation and wondered if, like a movie, a half dozen black sedans would descend on the place, spilling out Kevlar-armored shifters with guns, ordering her to give herself up.

The suburban street remained silent. No suspicious cars arrived, and at Everett's inclined head bob indicating the door, she strode back into his lair and hoped she hadn't made a mistake.

11

Spotting the uncertainty and fear painted on Dawn's face was easy, just like he could read the confusion and curiosity on Tom's. For some reason, putting Dawn at ease seemed more important at the moment than appeasing his friend.

Depositing their purchases on the counter, he acted as if everything was fine. He wasn't about to allow Tom, or anyone else for that matter, to turn Dawn in.

"Why don't you put the dry staples away while I clear out the fridge," he offered, dumping out a grocery bag and letting its contents roll on the counter. With the empty bag in hand, he headed to the dreaded ice box and prepared himself to battle the mold.

"I don't know where anything goes," she replied, her nose still twitching with wariness, but at least the tension in her was no longer strung tauter than an acoustic wire. As for Tom, he held his tongue for the moment as he sat down in a chair and snagged a banana to munch on. Silent, he watched them, but Everett could imagine he had a mouthful to say.

"Put it anywhere. It's what I do."

"Why am I not surprised?" she muttered. She took items and began placing them on shelves while Everett's arm swept the contents on his fridge shelves into the bag. Make that bags. It took three to rid it of the spoiled items.

"So, Tom, how was your night?" he asked in a carefree, conversational tone.

"Oh, you know, same old, same old. I went home. Ate. Slept. Came to work. Found my partner consorting with a wanted criminal."

Everett winced, and Dawn froze. "Who says she's a criminal?"

"I might be slow, but I'm not an idiot. You weren't the only one who read the FUC fax. Anyone care to explain why you have a psychotic shifter in your house?"

"I'm not psychotic." Dawn planted her hands on her hips.

"At the moment," Tom countered. "Unlike my friend over here, I did my research. While you might seem currently normal, it's been well established at this point that all those who got the injection from Mastermind have turned into raving lunatics."

"I haven't."

"Yet. But what happens if I eat the last cookie, or someone looks at you the wrong way?"

"You forgot to add PMS to that list."

"I didn't forget. I've dated enough to know all women are crazy when that hits."

"I'm not a killer."

"And I'm supposed to just accept your word about that when I've got a whole agency telling me otherwise?" Tom stubbornly stuck to his stance.

"I won't let you turn me in." Dawn and Tom faced off.

Everett found himself in the odd and new situation of acting as referee. "Everybody needs to calm down."

"I am calm," Dawn stated. "But I don't like the fact your friend here is calling me crazy and accusing me of acts that never crossed my mind. Although, in his case, I might make an exception."

"Just stating facts." Tom shrugged.

"The fact is, Dawn saved me," Everett stated.

"She tied you to a bed and left you to starve."

"I did not. I knew Everett would escape. Eventually."

"So you're not as murderous as some of the others being hunted. It doesn't change the fact you're a wanted woman, and we're in the business of turning wanted people in. Or has our job description changed?" Tom asked, directing the last bit at Everett.

"No. We're still bounty hunters for hire. But,"—he held up a hand to forestall Tom—"for my own reasons, I've chosen not to turn Dawn in, on the condition she stays with me and lets me keep an eye on her. She's also agreed to help us find the shifter that threw me off the cliff. The one I was originally hunting when I came across her."

"And how is this little doe supposed to help us?"

Good question. Everett wasn't quite sure of that

part, but he did know, despite Tom's feelings on the matter, he wasn't comfortable handing her off to FUC.

Thankfully, Dawn knew how to help herself. "I think I know where the creature is hiding out."

"You do?"

She bobbed her head. "Like I said before. I was aware Joey was living in the park with me, just like he seemed to know I was kicking around. Unless he's moved locations, I'm pretty sure I can guide you to his hideout."

"Let me guess, it's remote."

"Well, yes."

Tom shook his head. "And you expect us to just follow you there, trusting little lambs, where you can then turn into a crazy monster, kill us both, and hide our bodies."

"What? Not going to add in a bit of cannibalism there? I do, after all, really enjoy my red meat since the incident." She clacked her teeth at Tom with a naughty smile.

The idea was so ludicrous Everett couldn't help himself. He laughed. And laughed. Until he caught Tom's glare, which made him snort. What did freeze his mirth, though, was the less than amused pursing of Dawn's lips. Hmm. With her eyes narrowed like that and her nostrils flaring, she did appear dangerous, to a household spider maybe.

Even if her animal does have a bit of a violent side, I'm sure my wolf can handle it.

"I am going on the record as saying I think this is a bad idea," Tom announced.

"Duly noted." And ignored. Everett lost count of the

bad ideas he'd indulged in his lifetime. Unlike Tom, he knew not all of them ended in disaster.

With Tom agreeing to keep FUC out of their plans for the moment, they came to an uneasy truce. They didn't depart on the hunt that day, but they did plan. This time, Everett was going in better armed and informed. While Dawn entertained herself cleaning his house, and Tom shot him disgusted looks in between digging up more information, Everett made some calls and ordered the equipment he needed. Problem was, they couldn't deliver it for a day or so, which meant he got to spend the evening with one hot doe—and a chaperoning sloth.

"What do you mean you're staying?" Everett hissed when Tom mentioned this fact in passing as he eased himself into the La-Z-Boy chair in his living room.

"As your best and only friend, the task to protect you falls upon me."

"From what?"

Tom didn't say a word, just cast a glance at the kitchen, where they could hear the dangerous female in question. She hummed as she brandished her plastic spatula making who knew what, but damn did it smell good.

"Seriously, dude? Dawn won't hurt me."

"Good. It will my make my task easier then."

"You don't have to stay. I'll be fine." Not to mention having Tom around would cramp his plans. Cock-blocking was not cool.

"What kind of friend would I be if I didn't? I'd never forgive myself if I came back in the morning and found you dead."

"Of what?"

"I don't know. And neither do you. You don't know this girl. Who knows what she's capable of?"

Everett rolled his eyes. "She's a freaking doe. What's she going to do, ask me to hold still so she can trample me with her little hooves?"

"She could poison you."

Mmm. If that's what poisoning smelled like, at least he'd die happy with a full belly. "So we watch her eat whatever she's concocting first."

"She could kill you in your sleep."

"She could have done that last night when I staggered home drunk, yet she chose not to."

"So she's sane when in human form. What if she suddenly shifts?"

"Then I contain her until she regains her senses."

Tom made a noise of disgust. "You have an answer for everything."

"Because your worries are groundless, and you know it. What's this really about?"

"You're not acting like yourself."

"What do you mean not acting like myself?"

"Well, for one thing, you brought a woman back to your place. You never bring them home."

True. He preferred to keep his home address private ever since the stalking incident with Mary-Jane a few years back. Not to mention, the usual messy state of his home didn't make for a romantic ambiance. "I don't bring one-night-stands home. This is different. I needed her close to keep an eye on her."

"Which brings me to my second point. You didn't turn her in and collect the bounty."

"Only because she can help me bring in a more dangerous suspect."

"Since when do you need or want help?"

"I don't know, which makes me wonder what I'm paying you for. Are you done?"

"No. You took her shopping."

"And?"

"Shopping. For food. You hate going to the store. You don't care what's in your cupboards, and you certainly don't give a damn that your place is a pig sty."

"Hey, I resent that. I saw how the three pigs lived and let me tell you I did the world a favor when I blew that place down."

"You're letting her clean your house."

"In exchange for a place to stay and a paycheck. And, trust me, given what I can afford, she's getting screwed."

"Dude, you won't even let your mother do that!"

"Shh. Keep your voice down."

"Shh? Did you seriously shh me? And you wonder why I'm worried? Did she magically entrance you with her pussy?"

"Dawn's not that kind of girl." A pity.

"So why are you acting like this? Is it because she won't let you in her pants? Is that it? You find a fugitive who won't let you screw her and suddenly you're tossing your morals out the window?"

Everett scratched his scalp. "Since when do I have morals?"

An actual growl passed Tom's lips. "And this is why I'm not leaving. It's for your own good."

"Whatever. You want to stay, then stay, but I don't

know where you think you're sleeping. I already gave her the bed."

"Are you trying to make me believe you actually slept on the couch last night?"

"Well, um…"

Tom's unibrow lifted.

Everett sighed. "Okay, so maybe I didn't. But I meant to! I accidentally ended up in bed with her. However, it should be noted she didn't want me there. She made me promise to sleep out here, but I kind of forgot when I got drunk last night."

A snort of disgust blew past Tom's lips. "You're hopeless."

"Finally someone who agrees with me," Dawn announced, appearing in the archway leading to the kitchen. "Now, if you're done discussing me and the evil I'm plotting, shall we eat? I promise you won't taste the arsenic."

With a bright smile at Tom, Dawn pivoted and headed back to the kitchen.

Tom at least had the decency to look abashed.

"Ha," Everett exclaimed. "You got caught slamming the cook. I hope she spit in your portion."

"One of these days, wolf…"

"What, ol' buddy?"

"You know what, I hope she does turn into a freaky killer and rips your dick off and eats it."

Anything involving her mouth and his cock sounded good to him. *Awooo!*

12

Dawn should have probably been more offended at Tom's remarks, which she couldn't help but overhear given her sensitive auditory senses. He didn't trust her at all and made no bones about it. She didn't like that he'd judged her without knowing her, but she couldn't disagree with a lot he said. Not the poisoning part, of course—she wouldn't ruin good food like that—but the rest, she couldn't argue.

Was she capable of violence? Possibly. She definitely wasn't the girl she used to be. Just look at what the injection had done to her once beautiful doe. Sob. But, no, she wouldn't think about that now.

What she did ponder, though, was Everett's staunch defense of her. Why didn't he turn her in? Why did he seem convinced she wouldn't harm him or anyone else? She couldn't deny she'd changed, that she harbored something inside her that wasn't soft and fluffy. Something dark. Something that enjoyed red meat and wanted to hunt.

She fought an inner battle against these alien sensations, a battle that made her wonder if she wasn't better off turning herself in at times. What if she did end up hurting someone? *And, worse, what if I enjoy it?*

As they sat around the dinner table, she could see Tom eyeing the bowl and platter set in the middle of it. She sighed.

"Oh for Pete's sake. I didn't poison it. Here. Watch." She spooned a large portion of the rice with stir-fried vegetables onto her plate and dumped some of the teriyaki-style chicken on top of it. She dug in, each forkful a heavenly bite after eating out of a can for so long. It wasn't entirely for Tom's benefit she moaned. It tasted damned good.

Apparently, she passed the dubious sloth's test. He helped himself and dug in with gusto, his only concession to her culinary skills the occasional grunt. As for Everett, he'd not hesitated and scarfed down his repast and his second helping before they'd even finished their first.

At the end of their meal, he leaned back in his chair and patted his belly. He also belched, more than once.

"Excuse me," she said with a pointed glare in his direction.

"Excuse you for what?"

"Not me, you. Or did your mother not teach you any table manners?"

"Sure she did. Don't chew with your mouth open. No throwing food. Oh, and if you don't like what's on your plate, starve."

"He's not serious, is he?" she asked, turning to Tom, who couldn't hide a smile.

"Oh, he's very serious. Trust me, burping is one of the more polite things he could have done."

"You mean there's worse?"

"Hey," the wolf in question protested. "Where I come from, burping is considered a compliment to the chef."

"Next time, I'd prefer you use words," she admonished, grabbing the empty plates and carrying them to the sink.

"It was lovely," he stated in a mocking tone.

"It was the best home-cooked meal we've both had in a while," Tom grudgingly admitted.

Dawn beamed. "Really? In that case then, I guess you both deserve some of the apple pie I baked."

This time, they made sure to copiously compliment her once they polished it off. Tom might have started out doubting her culinary motives, but once he got over his fear of choking to death, he made up for it in lip-smacking enthusiasm. It almost brought a tear to her eye when they battled over the final piece.

The boys watched a football game on television and she hummed as she washed the dishes, the normality of it soothing. How easy to imagine the horror of the past few months as nothing more than a mirage. How easy to pretend this was her life, a simple housewife cooking and cleaning for her wolf before retiring for the night and…

Whoa. She reined in her fantasy. She needed to remind herself that this wasn't real. She and the wolf weren't a couple. The situation was temporary at best. For the moment, she might find herself safe, but one wrong move and she didn't doubt they'd turn her in and collect their reward. The reminder sobered her.

When she'd cleaned everything, and delayed as long as possible, she dithered, wondering what to do. Should she go to bed? Join them in the living room? Escape while they were relaxed and not paying attention?

"Penny for your thoughts."

She screamed at the whispered words and jabbed an elbow back in reflex. Everett *oomphed* as she hit him square in the diaphragm. "Oops. Sorry. You startled me."

"I'll say," he gasped. "Lucky me, you didn't aim lower."

"Maybe you shouldn't have snuck up on me like that."

"Sure, blame the victim."

"Suck it up, puppy," Tom yelled from the living room.

Everett rolled his eyes. "Thanks for your sympathy."

Tom laughed, and Dawn couldn't help but smile.

"Are you going to join us in the living room?"

"I think I should go to bed. I'm kind of tired."

"Want some company?"

She'd love some company. Him, her, the bed, and no clothes. Just one teensy tiny problem. She knew it was a bad, very bad, idea. Thank goodness for Tom. At least he had the good sense to realize it, and his presence made it easy for her to shake her head. She ignored the disappointment in Everett's eyes as she fled. He'd get over it. A man like him probably wasn't used to hearing the word no. *He'd better get used to it because no way am I becoming another notch on his belt, no matter what my wet panties think.*

Why the wolf attracted her so strongly, she couldn't say. Was it because of the changes within her? Did his dangerous side attract the predator in her? *It could be because he's so darned good-looking.*

Whatever the reason, getting involved definitely wasn't part of her plan.

She sighed. A shame, though. Being a part of something, even something as dysfunctional as this situation, was better than being alone. She'd forgotten the enjoyment of conversing with others. Of the pleasure that came with cooking for an appreciative audience. She'd especially missed companionship of the male kind, the flirting, tummy-tingling feeling that came about when an attractive male sniffed around and made his interest known.

If only they'd met in a different time and place. If only she had somewhere else to go, somewhere she wouldn't have to deal with all the confusion mounting in her mind.

For some reason, her thoughts turned to her family. After her initial rescue from Mastermind's clutches, she'd contacted her parents to let them know she was safe. She downplayed the danger, especially once she realized they'd heard little to nothing about Mastermind. What was the point in worrying them? She'd escaped relatively unscathed. They didn't need to know the gory details.

When she escaped a second time, this time from FUC, she'd made one collect call, only to have her mother demand to know where she was and why the authorities were looking for her. Her dad wanted her to do the right thing and turn herself in. Her mother blamed her troubles on her lack of morals since she'd gone to the big city. And as for Grandma... Grandma told her to run and not look back.

So she did. But what Grandma didn't tell her, and Dawn quickly discovered, was running took a lot of energy. Not just that, but it was lonely. Used to living in a herd, she found the solitary life hard to adjust to. Probably the reason why she didn't fight the wolf for long when he insisted on keeping her close. Even associating with the big, bad wolf appealed more than listening to the crickets every night.

The door to the bedroom opened on silent hinges, but the light from the hall illuminated the room for a moment, and she saw Everett slip in.

"What are you doing here?" she whispered.

"I can't sleep out there."

"Why ever not?"

He held open the bedroom door again, and she opened her mouth to query again when she heard it. A wet, rolling rumble followed by a whistle.

"What is that?"

"Tom."

"Good grief. That's noisy."

"Hence my request to sleep in here. I promise I'll behave."

"Ha. Like I'll believe that."

"Okay, how about I won't do anything you don't want?"

Not much better since she wanted so many things

from him, hot and sweaty naked things she couldn't have. "Isn't there anywhere else you can go?"

"I guess I could sleep in the bathroom tub."

Picturing him lolling in the tub, long limbs dangling over the side brought a snicker to her lips.

"Not funny," he grumbled. "I'm going to need my sleep if we're going hunting for the giant gecko tomorrow."

"If I do agree, do you promise to stick to your side of the bed?"

"Scout's honor."

She couldn't hold back a snort. "You were never a scout."

"No, but I scared quite a few in my heyday."

Before she could change her mind, he'd slipped into bed. She turned her back to him with a mumbled goodnight and clamped her eyes tight. The bed wiggled and wobbled as he squirmed on his side until finally she said, "Would you stop that?"

"Sorry. I should have gotten undressed before climbing in."

What? She rolled over and ogled him. "I said no hanky-panky."

"I know."

"So why are you stripping?"

"To get comfortable of course." His tone eloquently said, "Duh!"

She should have left it at that, but suddenly, all she could think of was the fact Everett didn't wear underwear, which meant he was...

"You're naked?"

"It's how I sleep."

"Couldn't you make an exception given we have to share the bed?"

"But then I wouldn't be comfortable."

She could almost see his pout. "Am I supposed to care?"

"Aw, come on, little doe. What's the big deal? I mean, it's not like you're planning to take advantage of me, are you?" He sounded almost hopeful.

"You wish."

"What a shame. I was totally willing to let you ravish me."

"You're incorrigible."

"But sexy, right?"

Sexy didn't even come close. He was the ultimate temptation. *One I intend to resist.* She inched as close as she could to her edge of the mattress. "Stay on your side."

"No worries here, little doe. I am a wolf of my word. But are you sure you're capable of keeping your hands off me? As I recall, last time we shared a bed, I woke to you fondling me."

She rolled over to glare at him. "I was not fondling you."

"Sure you weren't." His placating tone only agitated her further.

With a muttered expletive about "horny wolves in need of muzzles and castration," she turned her back to him and tried to go to sleep.

She remained much too aware of him.

She tried counting sheep. She got to twelve before a naked Everett on all fours appeared chasing them.

Blanking her mind of all thought also failed. His

mocking grin kept drifting up from the depths of her subconscious.

Agitated and in a heightened state of awareness, she punched her pillow and yanked the covers to cocoon herself more tightly.

"Something wrong, little doe? You seem awfully restless."

"I'm fine," she muttered. Just aroused. And she wasn't about to go back on her stance and have him fix that.

"I can't sleep either. Wanna talk?"

"About?"

"You."

"I'm not very interesting."

"Then we'll talk about me because I am super awesome."

She wouldn't have labeled him as such, but he sure was entertaining. As she listened to him recount tales of his life growing up in a family of wolves, a pack with five boys and one wooden spoon-wielding mother, she found herself opening up. When he told her of the time he'd singed the fur off his tail because his brother tied firecrackers to it for the Fourth of July, she found herself recounting the time she'd painted stripes on her brother so he could be a zebra for Halloween—with acrylic, not water-based paint.

The soothing cadence of Everett's voice eased her, and next thing she knew, her eyes fluttered shut and she slipped into the sleep that previously eluded her.

And, this time, when she woke atop the wolf to him nibbling on her neck, she didn't scream or maim him in any way. But when he suggested they celebrate the dawn with a quickie, she did twist his nipple until, with a howl, he agreed to fetch her some Starbucks.

For those who wondered, no, she didn't look away when he rolled out of bed and strutted naked to his dresser, his taut buttocks flexing. Like a beautiful sunset, some things were meant to be admired.

13

WHAT A VIEW, and Everett didn't mean the leaves that garnished boughs in a rainbow of color. He also didn't refer to the distant mountain range, their peaks bathed in a wispy fog. Nope. What he enjoyed was smack dab in front of him, clad in snug jeans with a plaid shirt—his, he might add. With the shirt tails tucked in to her snug jeans, he got a clear view of Dawn's sweet ass as it wiggled this way and that. It made a man want to go on a nature hike more often. What a shame this one wasn't leading to a sunny, grass-filled glade with a blanket, but instead to a murderous gecko's lair.

If ever they came out this way again, for pleasure instead of work, he really should try and get her to wear a skirt, a short and loose one, with a thong. Mmm. He practically panted at the visual image.

A slap across the back of his head snapped him from his pleasant reverie.

"Pay attention," Tom growled.

"I am." He memorized every inch.

"To something other than her butt, you idiot."

"I am."

Tom *harrumphed.*

How dare he doubt me! Despite what Tom thought, Everett actually was keeping an eye and ear out. Hot buttocks or not, Everett was well aware they strode into danger. The occasional twinge of his not completely healed injuries made sure of that. He proved it to Tom. "Squirrels' nest at four o'clock. Fox tracks at nine, only a few hours old. There's water to the east, and a thicket of overripe raspberries to the north. Oh, and you need better deodorant."

Tom clamped his lips shut, and Everett smirked. Dawn didn't deign to even turn her head. Nor did she slow down or take any precautions, despite the fact they encountered more and more signs of something large having passed numerous times this way. Then again, perhaps like him, she smelled the fact that none of the gecko tracks were more recent than a day or two. That combined with the fresher scents of forest animals crisscrossing the place without fear was enough to make his guard lower. But he still kept one hand on the butt of the gun slung around his hips. As for Tom, he carried a rifle in two hands, head swiveling to and fro, ready to take aim at the slightest provocation.

And people thought sloths were too lazy to hunt.

According to research, geckos liked a place to hide. Many chose to make their habitats in holes or crevices. In this case, their monstrous neighborhood gecko had taken over an abandoned cave as its own. That or he'd eaten the previous occupant. The maw into darkness oozed a fetid stench, and the three of them stood staring at the opening, nobody eager to be the first to set foot inside.

As alpha of the group, the task fell to him to set the example. Sometimes it sucked being the lead tracker. It meant he got to go into the funkiest places. Everett blew out a breath at the stench. "Damn. And I thought my place was a mess."

"It was," Dawn teased.

His glare her way just made her smile. *Hot pig on a stick, I am so screwed.* Her evident pleasure did things to his insides he'd rather not contemplate. For both their sakes, he really needed to do something about their sleeping situation; this whole sharing a bed thing was driving him nuts. A woman in his bed, especially one as sexy as Dawn, should involve little sleep and lots of sex. If he didn't do something soon, he'd probably explode, and then they'd take his man card away for not having any balls. But he'd deal with that problem later. Right now, they had a fetid cave to explore. "Tom, I want you keep watch while I check this place out."

"Better you than me."

To his surprise, Dawn stuck by his side as he entered the gecko's lair. She stepped gingerly among the trash—empty cans of pop, cellophane chip bags, a few shoes, scraps of cloth, and holy shit, was that the remnants of a black bear?

Her nose wrinkled as she looked around. "This is gross."

"Very."

"I did my part. I led you to Joey's home, now what?"

"We look for clues."

"Clues of what?" she asked. "The fact he might be distantly related to you given he's also not one to clean up after himself?"

"Ha. Ha. Aren't you just the funny one."

She smirked. "I try. Seriously, though. What do you think we'll find?"

"Hopefully something that will tell us where he's gone."

"Why don't we just conceal ourselves and wait for him to come back?"

"Because I don't think he plans to return," Everett announced, toeing through the garbage.

"And you can tell this because…" she prompted.

"For one thing, it's been at least a day, maybe two, since he's come here."

"I don't understand why that's a clue to his behavior."

"Simple. Look at the stuff around us. He obviously prefers to snag his food and bring it back to enjoy at his leisure."

"So he decided to eat al fresco."

"That's not all. Whatever he was using as a bed is gone. You can see the outline over here where he must have had a sleeping bag on the ground. It's missing. As well, I see a few pieces of clothing abandoned."

"So he doesn't like to eat his victims' outfits."

"Except these didn't belong to his victims. First off, there's no blood on them, and I highly doubt they'd let a monster strip them for dinner without a fight. Secondly, smell them."

"Do I have to?"

He ignored her expression of disgust and waved the discarded rags under her nose.

She sniffed. "They smell of lizard."

"Exactly. These belonged to him, but are dirty or torn. Rejects. I think our gecko prey has packed up his stuff and moved on."

"But to where?"

"That is the question."

"Well, he can't have too many places to go. I mean, people will notice a giant lizard walking around."

"Don't be so sure. When in his shifted form, he might be easy to spot, but if he's still able to retain a human shape and wear clothing and whatnot, he could blend in quite easily with humans."

"But we'd still smell him."

"We would if we could find him. Do you know where to look?"

She shook her head.

"And therein lies our dilemma."

"So you're just giving up?"

Everett barked out a laugh. "Give up? Like hell. Hunting criminals is what I do. Do you really think most of them stick around in their last known location waiting for me to pick them up? Hell no. Bounty hunting is about chasing them down. Figuring out where they're going, what they're going to do, and getting one step ahead of them."

"But Joey's not a regular criminal."

"He's got anger issues. Sooner or later, he's going to snap, or shift, and when he does surface, we'll have to make sure we're paying attention so we can nab him."

"In other words, someone else needs to get killed."

Everett shrugged. "Hopefully not. I don't suppose you know what, other than humans and bears, he likes to eat?"

She shook her head.

"Then it's back to my house we go for more research. There's got to be something in his file or on the Internet about geckos that will give us a clue. Maybe we'll get lucky and find out he's got a thing for IHOP pancakes. The only one for hundreds of miles around is only a few blocks from my place."

"Did someone say pancakes?" Tom popped his head into the cave.

"Gotta love a sidekick with selective hearing."

"Nothing wrong with my hearing. It's my tummy that likes to eavesdrop."

"Then what are we waiting for? If we get moving now, we can make it out before dusk. And get home in time for *Survivorman*."

Dawn snorted. "You don't seriously watch that, do you?"

"Love it. Do you know I was in one of the episodes? I was the wolf making him just about piss his pants in his lean-to one night. You can even see the glint of my eyes. Ma was so proud."

"You are so whacked."

"And I am so hungry, so if you're done yapping, can we get going?" Tom grumbled.

Fine with Everett. The faster they got back and ate, the quicker he could hopefully ditch Tom and get to work on getting a certain doe to lower her guard—and morals.

Awooo!

14

Up the street from the IHOP...

Joey twitched as he walked. He couldn't help it. A nervous man before his change, he'd become even more paranoid since his transformation.

Everyone's watching me. But they hid it well, averting their gazes when he peered suspiciously at them. The tin foil hat he'd fashioned to prevent the FUC agency from beaming into his brain waves did nothing to prevent the humans from suspecting there was something special about him. Just like his humble clothes couldn't mask his greatness.

Once so low on the totem pole of shifters, Joey had skipped several rungs on the evolutionary ladder when Mastermind gifted him with her magic potion. Where once he'd reviled the rodent who caged him, now he posthumously thanked her. He would have to remember to thank the FUC agents who made his change possible, right before he ate them. His tummy rumbled.

Goober on a stick, he was starving. The last thing he'd eaten was a family of raccoons, hours ago. His empty belly gurgled again, expressing its discontent. It would have to wait. Before he took care of his increased dietary requirements, he needed to do something about his appearance. His shining greatness was drawing too much attention.

When he'd first escaped FUC custody, covered in blood and high on the adrenaline of the kill, he'd pounced on the first human about his size he'd come across. A naked blood-smeared man running around the city tended to attract notice almost as much as a giant murderous gecko. The human male he chose to rob didn't survive—broken necks tended to be fatal—and neither did his wardrobe. The victim's wallet yielded an address, and a pocket coughed up some keys.

After dumping the naked body in a dumpster, Joey used his acquired goods to raid his victim's apartment, clothing himself, taking what he could to pawn, and buying himself a train ticket out of the city. Not as far as he would have liked, but distant enough he didn't have to worry about running into FUC every time he turned around. Or so he'd hoped when he'd ended up in boony land.

For a while, he'd hidden in the protected parkland, feasting like a gecko king on campers and wildlife, stealing picnic baskets like a favorite cartoon character and hiding out in a cool cave, just like Batman. And then there was his favorite indulgence, spying on Dawn.

Sigh. He loved thinking of Dawn. So delicate. So perfect. So ladylike. His idea of a perfect mate and woman.

Until that stupid wolf came along and ruined it all.

It wasn't enough the mangy mutt had found Joey and compromised his hunting ground, he'd taken Dawn. Took her! Away from the forest and away from Joey.

He didn't like that part one bit. Sure, he'd not technically declared his love and intentions to the soft-eyed doe, but only because he was shy. *I was still working up the nerve to ask her out.*

But now, with that nosy wolf on the scene, he didn't stand a chance. Poor Dawn was his prisoner. Forced to leave with the smelly canine. Torn away from her destiny. *Me.*

Despite the setback, he wasn't giving up. Somehow, some way, he'd find out where the dastardly wolf kept his one true love prisoner, and he'd free her from the hairy beast. And Dawn, also one of the lucky ones given the change, would be so happy at being rescued she'd fall in love with Joey and they'd live happily ever after.

That or he'd eat her. He'd always wondered what venison tasted like.

15

Over food, they discussed their next plan of attack.

"I say we stake out the entrances to the park," Tom said between mouthfuls of fluffy pancakes smothered in whipped cream and chocolate sauce.

Everett snorted. "Oh, yeah, because the gecko is so law abiding, he's just going to park in a designated spot and hike on in. Come on, Tom. You've been doing this as long as I have. Do you really think that's going to work?"

"Where else can he hunt and hope to get away with it? Hikers go missing all the time in these parts. It's why they have the big signs all over the place warning campers to beware and not feed the wild animals."

"And I'm telling you, he's not going back. He knows we're onto him."

"So what makes you think he's even still in the area? What's to stop him from hopping on a bus to anywhere? If Joey knows you're looking for him, then wouldn't he move to the next town or forest?"

Dawn queried as she nibbled on her whole wheat toast, all that was left of her country fried steak and egg breakfast. She'd pounced on the grub as soon as her plate arrived. It was all Everett could do to keep up. Who would have thought a woman with such a healthy appetite would be such a turn-on?

"It's a possibility. But, if there's one thing I know, it's predators." Everett flashed some teeth. "We don't like ceding territory to anyone, especially not other males. If this Joey character has any testosterone in him, then he's not going anywhere. On the contrary, I'd even go so far as to wager he's looking for me."

"But he thinks he killed you."

"He didn't see me die. First rule of being a predator, unless you've seen them take their last breath, then never assume the enemy is dead."

"He'll still have the same problem as us, though, how to find you. I mean, it's not as if you can take an ad out in the paper and say, hey, crazy gecko monster, I live at—"

"Hot damn. That's it! You're brilliant, little doe."

Dawn blinked as she rewound the conversation and still ended up with a blank. "Excuse me? I think I missed something."

"You're right. I need to get his attention. Tell him exactly where he can find me."

"But how?"

"By doing something spectacular enough to make the front page news."

"In other words, by being an idiot," Tom added.

"Shouldn't be too hard," she muttered.

Tom guffawed, and Everett glared. "Ha. Ha. You are both so funny."

"Thank you," she replied primly as she leaned over and stole his last piece of toast. "So what spectacular thing are you going to do to make yourself get noticed? Because I don't think conceit will get you on the front page of the paper."

"No, but solving a case, or doing something cool and heroic will."

Tom tried to interject some reason. "You can't stage a rescue."

"Says who?"

"I'm with Tom on this one. Acts of heroism are usually random. You can't plan them."

"That's what you think."

Less than two hours later...

How did I end up roped into this crazy plan?

Strutting down the sidewalk, in front of the newspaper office for the town, where a light shone in the window as the editor worked on the last-minute items before sending the paper to print, Dawn swung her overlarge and bulging purse.

This is never going to work. But it wouldn't be because they hadn't tried. The plan they'd concocted was ridiculous; however, Everett wouldn't allow himself to be swayed so, with a shrug, she and Tom agreed. They gathered their supplies and now put the plot in motion.

Footsteps rushed in behind her. She fought the urge

to glance over her shoulder. *Just act natural. Be a victim. Shouldn't be too hard.* Deer, after all, weren't considered predators to anything except vegetation and gardens. *Watch out, romaine lettuce, or I will tear you apart!*

Biting her lip so as to not burst into hysterical giggles, she managed an authentic scream when her purse got yanked off her shoulder. The snatcher darted past her, swinging it as he pounded the pavement. Just one problem. This stranger was not part of their plot for attention!

Annoyed at the young thug who sprinted away, foiling their inane scheme, Dawn kicked off her heels and bolted after him. "Thief!" she shouted. "You get back here with my purse. I need that."

The juvenile delinquent had the nerve to flash her the bird.

Oooh, he did not just do that. The old Dawn would have probably burst into tears. Old Dawn, being a law-abiding citizen would have rushed to the nearest police precinct and reported the crime. New Dawn, though? New Dawn got mad.

Adrenaline coursing through her at the temerity of the thief, Dawn sped after him, her bare feet slapping the concrete sidewalk.

The purse snatcher turned, and his eyes widened when he noted she'd just about closed the gap between them. She bared her teeth and growled, "I said give it back."

He had the nerve to say, "Like hell, you crazy lady!"

Crazy, huh? She showed him no mercy. Launching herself, she tackled him. Down they went, her atop the thug, his body providing a cushion for their hard landing on the pavement. Jabbing her knee in his spine to keep him down, she grabbed the arm with her purse and twisted it behind his back before she harangued him. "What is wrong with you? Stealing from women? Didn't your mother teach you any better? Well?" she snapped tersely when the delinquent didn't reply.

A flash went off, temporarily blinding her, and it was that image that went viral, not just in the morning edition of the paper, but everywhere. Overnight, she became a YouTube sensation as someone who'd caught footage of the chase posted it. She also made the front page news.

Dawn groaned when she read the article the next day over breakfast.

Local Resident Takes Down Serial Purse Snatcher

Dawn Johnson, wife of Everett Johnson, owner and bounty hunter for Lone Wolf Agency, took down Juno Smith last night, teaching the youth that not all women are easy prey...

The article went on at length about her heroic act and bravery. They even had a picture of the cops shaking her hand for helping them catch the wanted criminal.

Everett sulked at the breakfast table as he pushed around the scrambled eggs on his plate. "I can't believe our plan got screwed."

"I don't see what the problem is," she said as she sipped at her coffee. "You wanted us to do something to get noticed. We got noticed."

"But I was supposed to be the hero." His disgruntlement at not being the star of the show showed clearly.

Men! They could be such babies sometimes. "Get

over it. You're a wolf. You should be used to being the bad guy."

"First off, I am really tired of the stereotype."

"Says the guy who uses it to his advantage whenever he can."

"And secondly," he continued as if he'd not heard her, "what on earth possessed you to tell them we were married?"

Dawn choked on her coffee. "Yeah. Sorry about that. When they asked my name, I panicked. I didn't want to give them my real last name, and the first one I could think of was yours. Is it my fault they assumed we were a couple?"

"You didn't correct them."

"I don't see the big deal. I got your name and the agency in the article. Wasn't that the whole point?"

"And now thousands of women think I'm off the menu."

She snorted. "You're worried about your ability to get laid?"

Tom, who'd remained silent up to this point as he read the paper and ate, jumped in. "Actually, Everett, this might work in your favor. Lots of women find married guys attractive, but now you have an excuse not to get serious."

"You are not helping," Everett growled.

"Besides, you've got more important things to worry about than whose face got in the paper and your new marital status. Some FUC agents called and left a message on our office machine. Apparently, a pair of them are in town, and they want to meet with us to discuss the ongoing shifter hunt."

Before Dawn could bolt from her chair to the back door as self-preservation kicked in, Everett clamped a hand on her arm and held her down. "Sit. There's no need to panic and jump to conclusions. We don't know that they're here about you."

"They must have seen the article. They're probably here to take me down." She almost hyperventilated as she couldn't help but imagine the worst-case scenarios.

"Considering they asked to meet Everett and me at a local pancake house, I doubt it," Tom replied. "So don't get your panties in a knot just yet."

"What if that's just to throw us off? What if they're surrounding the house as we speak?" Dawn's eyes darted to the nearest window and peered with suspicion at the patch of bare grass studded with weeds that comprised Everett's backyard.

"I hardly doubt they'd warn us they were here if they planned to arrest you," Tom remarked dryly. "Use your head, doe, for something other than a wig rack."

Dawn glared at Tom, who simply ignored her.

"When do they want to meet?" Everett asked.

"In about a half hour."

"We'd better get ready then." Everett stood, but something about the way Dawn kept eyeing the back door with longing must have tipped him off that she still considered flight.

"Don't you even think of it, little doe."

"I won't just sit around and wait for them to show up to arrest me."

"No one's arresting you. And, even if they did, I'd call in some favors and make sure you got a fair shake."

"How reassuring." Her sarcasm came through loud and clear.

Everett dropped to his knees beside her and caught her gaze. "I mean it, Dawn. No one's going to hurt you. Not if you trust me and stay put while we go listen to what they say. Run, though, and they'll assume you're guilty and come after you, possibly with guns blazing."

"Your pep talk skills suck."

"Just being honest."

"For once," Tom muttered.

"Trust me."

Peering into his eyes, she could see he meant what he said. He wouldn't let them harm her. Big, bad wolf or not, his word meant something, and she was tired of running. She nodded.

"Good girl. We'll be back as soon as we can."

"With a doggie bag?"

"Filled with Danishes," he solemnly promised.

Off to the pancake house Everett and Tom went to meet with the FUC agents while Dawn remained at his home, alone, bored, and out of things to clean.

The floors in every room sparkled, and while they could use a coat of wax, they at least no longer wore a layer of clutter. All of the dishes were washed and put away. His bathroom was sterilized to the point a person could have eaten off the floor. Laundry was on the go, and she had meat marinating for dinner.

Not a fan of television, and with nothing to read or anyone to cook for, Dawn moped. *I understand why he couldn't bring me, but this whole waiting thing sucks.* A part of her would have preferred to be in on the action, to know what was going on.

Sure, he did her a favor by not letting the FUC agents see her. Still, though, after the excitement of the last few days, hanging by herself just didn't have the same thrill. The very idea froze her.

Since when do I need a thrill? Wasn't she the one who used to advocate a calm life? Who argued the only thing she wanted was a white picket fence-existence, free of mini masterminds and monsters and horny wolves who hit on her every time they shared the same breathing space?

Is the fact I miss the hairy womanizer another symptom of my madness, or something more serious? Something more dangerous than the arousal she couldn't seem to stem around him. *Don't tell me I'm falling for him?*

He'd probably run, howling on four legs, if he suspected it.

The doorbell rang, and she wondered who it could be. Everett and Tom obviously wouldn't ring for entry. What if it was FUC agents? Had they come to arrest her while the coast was clear?

What if it wasn't? She needed to control her paranoia. Not everything that happened revolved around her. According to Everett, the world revolved around him.

The clock showed the time as eleven thirty-three. Prime time for door-to-door salesmen looking to prey on housewives. Heck, it could even be a reporter. She was, after all, a star now. A star who now needed to keep her head down. In that case, she should stay out of sight and let whoever it was think no one was at home.

But what if it was Joey? Hadn't they done their media stint in the hope of flushing him? Maybe if he showed up, she could talk him into turning himself in without the need for violence. Promise him help for his condition so no one else needed to die.

Once it occurred to her, it became almost an imperative need to peek through the spyhole. *Must look. Can't resist.*

A lone, distinctly unattractive woman—and probably not one of Everett's conquests—stood on the stoop, not Joey. Forget answering. Everett very specifically told her to stay out of sight. But the female at the door wasn't very big, or scary-looking, or well dressed either. Wringing her hands and casting worried glances up and down the street, she appeared nervous. Dawn couldn't help but wonder if she needed help.

Indecision had her gnawing her lip. *How would I feel if I went to someone for help and no one bothered to listen?*

Her conscience won over common sense and Everett's orders. If it turned out the stranger outside was a reporter, Dawn would politely answer a few questions and then send her on her way. Pasting a smile on her lips, Dawn opened the door. A strong waft of perfume assailed her. She tried not to gag or wave her hand in front of her nose. Had the woman bathed in it?

"Can I help you?"

"Oh my," tittered the stranger. "I was hoping for a big strong man. My car has a flat tire."

"Sorry, but my, um, friend isn't here at the moment."

"Will he be back soon?"

Dawn shrugged. "Who knows?"

"Dear me. What shall I do?"

"Would you like to use my phone and call a repair service or something?"

"If it's not too much trouble."

"Hold on while I get the phone."

Dawn had only taken a few steps when the door behind her slammed shut. Trepidation tickled up her spine as she spun around on a heel. The ugly woman stood in the front entrance, except she wasn't quite a woman. Or so the wig being peeled from the bald head indicated. Glasses got flung to the side and…

Uh-oh. Even under the heavy, ill-applied makeup, she now recognized who she faced. *Our plan to get someone's attention worked.*

"Joey." She acknowledged him, and he beamed, his less-than-sane smile with its rouged lips creeping her right out.

"Yes, my dearest Dawn. It is I, come to save you from the vile clutches of the wolf."

Vile clutches? Somehow, she didn't get the impression her old prison mate had come looking for assistance. "Oh." More like a big fat uh-oh. "Um, thanks. But I don't need saving. As you can see, I'm perfectly fine. Great, actually." She inched backward toward the kitchen, where an array of knives sat on the counter. She also mentally slapped herself in the forehead with several "duhs" for falling into the classic trap of a stupid, trusting woman. Maybe she'd ask Everett to punish her later, if she got a later.

"No need to pretend in front of me. The wolf is gone. I saw him leave a while ago. We're alone. You can speak freely."

"You've been watching us?" Creepier and creepier.

Joey didn't seem to note her less-than-pleased response. He bobbed his head, looking more like a parrot in the moment than a gecko. "I found you last night after seeing your story on the evening news. How dare he mislead everyone into thinking you were his wife? I know he brought you here against your will, trying to keep us apart."

Creepier and creepier. "Us?"

"Yes, my dearest Dawn." Joey took a step forward, his expression fervent, and frightening. "I know I never said anything before, but surely you've felt it too. The instant connection. The lust. The rightness."

Hmm, yes, she had, just not for Joey. But somehow, explaining that didn't seem like the right thing to do at the moment, not if she planned to survive this encounter. She opted for a change of subject. "I'm actually here getting his help in negotiating with FUC. We're on their most wanted list. If we turn ourselves in, apparently they can help us." Okay, so she lied. She wasn't about to let on that, given Joey's crimes, he'd be lucky if he didn't end up skinned and turned into a handbag.

"Help? I don't need help, nor do I intend to let FUC get their hands on me. I like who I am."

"You're a giant lizard monster." Possibly not the most diplomatic way of putting it, but she wondered if bluntness might prevail where doefooting wasn't.

He didn't take offense. Rather, he beamed. "Isn't it marvelous? I went from being a nobody, a harmless little pet afraid of just about every other shifter out there, to someone they fear. Why would I want to give that up?"

She pointed out the obvious flaw. "Because you're killing people."

"I was hungry."

So much for rational logic. "Well, you should have hit a McDonald's instead of dining out on campers. That kind of thing draws attention. There's a warrant out for your capture, dead or alive."

Out puffed his scrawny chest. "They can try. I'm not afraid."

"That's just it. You should be. These guys mean business. And they have guns. Lots of them. As a matter of fact, Everett's one of those hunting you. You should leave before he comes home and finds you here."

"Let him come. If that mangy dog had not taken a coward's path before and jumped off that cliff, I would have killed him. I can't believe he survived, the rotten cur. Because I failed to finish him off, he got his dirty claws on you. For that, I blame myself. But never fear, my four-legged love. I won't make the same mistake twice. Let the wolf come. I will rend him limb from limb and free you from his wretched clutches."

How to answer that? Cheering on Joey's plan seemed wrong, yet denying it would probably prove deadly. Where was a grumpy sloth with his shotgun when a girl needed a tie-breaker?

"There's really no need for violence." Although she would have dearly loved a weapon right about now.

"Have I shocked your delicate sensibilities? I do apologize. Sometimes my violent nature takes even me by surprise. But I want you to know, you never have to fear me, Dawn. I want to protect you." He smiled, an awful leering grin. Dawn couldn't help but shiver before it.

He's insane. And had obviously read some really bad prose. Who the hell talked like that?

"Shall we wait for the wolf in the living room, or would you prefer we adjourn somewhere more *comfortable*?" He waggled his lopsided brows, and Dawn couldn't take it anymore. Stomach churning with nausea and fear, she turned tail, making a dash for the kitchen.

She launched herself at the block of knives, knocking them over in the process. The sharp blades skittered across the counter. Scrabbling, she managed to close her trembling fingers around the handle of one. She turned and brandished it before her. Joey, who'd scurried after her, halted.

"What are you doing?"

"Stand back, or else," she threatened, waving the blade in his direction.

The confusion on Joey's face lasted only a moment before anger set in. "What are you doing, Dawn?"

"You need to leave."

"Not without you."

She shook her head. "I'm not going anywhere with you."

Wrong answer.

Nostrils flaring, and his left eye twitching, Joey took a step toward her. "Don't make me angry. I can't always control myself when I'm angry, and I don't want to hurt you."

"And I don't want to go with you. Please, Joey. I know it's the injection that's making you crazy like—"

"I. Am. Not. Crazy!" Joey's rouged lips twisted, and his eyes flared. His twitch jumped from his left eye to his right and back again. His skin began to ripple.

Eep! She hurriedly spoke in an effort to calm him. "Sorry. That came out wrong."

His skin settled back to its regular pallor, and his twitch eased. "So you don't think I'm crazy?"

"Of course not. I mean, hey, if the injections made you nuts, then wouldn't I be nuts too?" She threw him a wan smile.

"We're special."

Tin hat special. "Listen, all I meant was I know you're having a tough time adjusting. I am too."

"I'm not having any problems. I'm perfectly fine."

"People who are fine don't go around killing and kidnapping people." Once again, her mouth got away from her as she tried to reason with him. What a waste of breath.

"Why not? They're weaker than me."

"It's wrong. Not only that, but you're going to expose us to the humans."

"So what? Isn't it about time the world knew about us? Discovered our superiority? Once upon a time, I used to think Mastermind was a nutjob, but now I have to wonder if she wasn't on to something. We are the better species, and those of us gifted with the injection even more so. Why, I've gone from being bottom of the food chain to eating the food chain."

"You're going to get us all killed if you don't stop."

The tic returned. "No, I won't, but you might end up next on the menu if you don't stop irritating me." He took a step forward, and she brandished the knife she still held before her to halt him.

"Please don't come any closer. I don't want to hurt you."

Judging by the speed he twitched, he didn't appreciate her defensive posturing. "Be a good doe and put the knife down."

She shook her head.

"Now, Dawn, be reasonable."

She tightened her grip.

With a cry that was half scream of frustration, half growl of caged beast, Joey burst from his clothes and shed his humanity.

Forget reasoning. Frankengecko was back, and, boy, did he look mad.

And hungry.

"Eep!"

16

THE VERY PREGNANT FUC agent excused herself from the restaurant table and went to the bathroom, her partner and husband following, a good thing too because Everett had stopped paying attention several minutes ago. He couldn't shake the feeling that something was wrong. Really wrong. He drummed his fingers on the table as he stared out the window.

Tom noticed his distraction and nudged him. "Why aren't you paying attention?"

"I am." At Tom's raised brow, he amended, "I was. But I've got this nagging sensation."

"Nagging how? Like a need-to-pop-a-Tums-because-I-ate-too-much-deep-fried-food sensation? A crack-open-a-new-package-of-toilet-paper-because-I'm-going-to-clog-some-plumbing? Or the I-think-I-left-the-stove-on-at-home one?"

"None of the above. I think something's wrong with Dawn."

Tom slammed the table with a fist. "I knew it. I

knew we shouldn't have left that doe alone. She's probably halfway to Canada by now."

"She didn't escape. I think she's in danger." Everett rose and tossed a few bills on the table.

"Where are you going?"

"To check on her."

"On the basis of your gut?"

"Don't make fun. That instinct has saved our tails more than once."

"You know, they have this new technology out now known as a phone. Instead of running off on the basis of a tummy ache, you could just call her."

"I can't. I don't have a house phone, remember? And she doesn't own a cell."

"So you're just going to disappear in the middle of a meeting with FUC agents?"

"Yup."

The scowl on Tom's face deepened. "You know that's not going to make us look good."

Everett rolled his shoulders. "Like I care what they think."

A noisy breath rattled from Tom's lips. "Well, I do! Are you nuts? You can't do that."

"Why not? Tell them something came up that needed my attention. I'm sure you can handle them."

Tom pounded a fist on the tabletop, rattling the dishes. "Everett, this better not be your way of ditching me so you can get back to Dawn for a little tickle and squeak."

"Dude, we are not in grade school. Tickle and squeak? Really?"

"You know what I mean."

"I do. And trust me when I say that's not my intention." Although, if his hunch turned out wrong, it might be.

"I'm coming by as soon as the meeting is over." The warning was growled.

"Take your time." Everett winked before striding out of the restaurant. He wasn't kidding, though, about his gut. It urged him to hurry. To run. He did, jogging the few blocks to his house.

Funny how in a few short days he'd grown so attached to the doe, and it wasn't just because of her housekeeping skills or great cooking. Under her demure side hid a woman with a backbone of steel. She exuded femininity yet, at the same time, didn't allow herself to get pushed around. For a man like him, who usually hung out with women who used sex as a tool to get what they wanted and tears when they didn't, he found it refreshing. And frustrating.

How she kept holding out again his charm, he couldn't figure out. He could tell she found him attractive. His nose never lied, and yet, she wouldn't let herself succumb. Was Tom right? Was it the thrill of the forbidden that rendered her so attractive?

Only one way to find out. *I need to seduce the doe.*

Arriving at his house, all thoughts of seduction vanished. Outwardly, nothing seemed amiss. The windows were all intact. No strange cars sat in his driveway or on the street. The front door was closed. There were no spray painted messages screaming *"Die, you man-whore!"* All appeared quiet at the lair of the wolf. But the lingering stench of a perfume applied with a much-too-liberal hand hung in the air. Nothing he owned and nothing Dawn wore.

A stranger had come—he sniffed—and not left.

A crash from within had him slamming open his front door and charging inside. The cloying perfume permeated the air, along with the more worrisome underlying stench of lizard. A big lizard, he'd wager.

In my house!

He couldn't help the howl at the invasion of his space. Quick on the heels of that thought was, *Shit, where's Dawn?*

A female scream sounded, quickly cut off. More noise, that of a scuffle, led him to his kitchen, where he beheld the gecko in a half shift advancing on Dawn, who huddled behind his island, knife in hand.

"Get away!" she yelled, waving her weapon.

"Come withhhh me," lisped the monster.

"Never!"

"You heard the lady. Back off," Everett growled.

The gecko-man turned his head and flicked his tongue. He didn't appear surprised at his appearance, nor worried, which Everett found a tad bit emasculating. Most people had some kind of reaction when confronting an angry wolf, even in human form. Some shook in their socks, others blubbered, most ran, and those that didn't usually left puddles of yellow.

Not Joey the giant freak. Nope, he opened his mouth wide, lined with unnaturally long teeth, and shot a wad of goo at him. Like, gross.

Everett ducked, and whatever came out of the lizard splattered the wall behind him. Eew. "That better not leave a stain," he complained.

"How about we repaint the walls with your blood?" Joey offered, turning his back on Dawn and flexing claws in his direction.

"Red is not my color." Really, it wasn't. Blue, maybe a bit of green, brought out the best in him, but red? Nope.

"You should have left my precious Dawn alone," Joey grumbled.

"I'm not yours," she shouted.

"Yet."

Try like ever. Everett didn't like the possessive claim the lizard tried to place on Dawn, and his wolf enjoyed it even less. With a roar, he sprang, claws extending from his fingertips, teeth elongating in his mouth, his wolf pushing to take over so it could rend the enemy into pieces. *Time to find out if gecko is like snake and tastes like chicken.*

He'd forgotten how fast the bastard was, and strong. One swipe was all it took to detour his flight and send him crashing into the sideboard holding his microwave. His poor Ikea furniture didn't stand a chance. The pine cracked, and down they all went, Everett, microwave, and the ceramic jar shaped and painted like Cookie Monster. *Damn. That thing was a classic.* Not to mention, what a waste of Oreos.

Despite the destruction of his treat stash, Everett didn't let the setback keep him down. He sprang to his feet and noted Joey dragged Dawn by the arm toward the front hall and door. She'd lost her knife, or had it taken from her. Either way, she could only dig her heels in on the linoleum floor and flail at the implacable grip towing her. She didn't stand a chance.

Good thing the big, bad wolf was here to help her.

Even though Joey had only partially shifted, he sported a large tail. With it thrashing so temptingly in front of him, Everett couldn't resist. He pounced on it and sank his claws in.

The lizard screamed, and the appendage thrashed, whipping Everett from side to side. He held on. He also couldn't resist an, "Awooo!" of exhilaration, which turned into an "Aw shit!" as the tail snapped off and sent him flying. "What the hell?" As he stared at the still-twitching tail in his grasp, he restrained a shudder. Damn geckos and their built-in security. He'd forgotten they could shed their tails like skin.

Meanwhile, while he lay there pinning the discarded piece of flesh, his target got away, with his doe. He jumped to his feet and darted after them. Joey had made it to the front door, but wasn't having an easy time of it as Dawn fought him hoof and nail.

"Let go of me," she yelled. She curled her hands around the frame of the door and held on for dear life.

Joey tugged. Everett grabbed hold of her hands just as the lizard tore her away. He leaned the opposite way of the gecko.

"Hold on, little doe," he grunted. "I've got you."

More than ever, he cursed himself for not carrying a gun. In his defense, he'd never needed to in the past. It was a humbling experience to finally meet something bigger and stronger than his wolf. Even more frightening was the knowledge he didn't know if he would win this impromptu tug of war. Despite all his weight and strength, he was losing the challenge.

"Pull harder," cried Dawn. "Don't let him take me."

"I'm trying," soothed Joey. "Fear not, my gentle doe, I shall save you from the wolf."

Huh?

"Not you, you overgrown handbag," she screeched. "Come on, wolf. Put some muscle into it. Don't tell me you're going to let a fly-eating lizard kick your hairy butt."

Forget gentle Dawn. Fighting-for-her-life Dawn didn't mince words as she threatened and cajoled him into trying harder while the oblivious lizard kept promising to save her. If it wasn't for the sweat pouring into his eyes and stinging them, Everett would have wondered if he dreamed, except even he knew his subconscious would never have him losing to a household pet.

Help came unexpectedly in the form of one sloth, who actually arrived in the nick of time with a "Holy shit! It wasn't indigestion."

The new threat had the effect of getting Joey to let Dawn go abruptly. Everett tumbled back and hit the floor. A moment later, Dawn landed atop him.

Panting, and tongue practically lolling, he still managed to say, "Hey, baby, how you doing?"

17

With her arms sore, heart racing, and skin clammy with fear, it took Dawn a moment to realize Everett was trying to mimic a famous line from a sitcom based in the nineties.

"Now is not the time for corny pickup lines," she snapped. "Or lying around. He's getting away." Given Joey's speech on his undying love for her, Dawn didn't have any doubt if he escaped, he'd come back, for her.

"I'm on it." Setting her aside, Everett jumped to his feet and ran out the front door, where she could hear excited voices and then the crack of a gun. Once. Twice.

It wasn't followed by screaming. Chest heaving, she couldn't help the shakes that consumed her body as the adrenaline of the fight wore off and reality set in. *I almost got kidnapped by an obsessed, doe-stalking lizard intent on making me his Geckobride.* If she weren't so scared, she would have laughed.

But the throb in her body wouldn't let her laugh about it, not when she'd come so close to getting kidnapped. Only Everett's timely arrival prevented her from a fate probably worse than death.

She closed her eyes and took several deep breaths, trying to calm her racing heart. Footsteps approached, and she heard the rustle of fabric as someone knelt beside her. Expecting to see Everett, or Tom at the very least, she screamed when she opened her eyes and instead beheld a blonde stranger who beamed and waved.

"Wassup?" queried the woman. "I'm Miranda, FUC agent extraordinaire, here to save the day."

Dawn decided to point out the flaw in her statement. "Um, how are you saving the day if you're inside with me and the monster gecko is outside?"

Miranda's pert nose wrinkled. "Okay, so I sent my hubby after it. But I want it known that my bunny and I would have kicked its lizard butt if it weren't for this ginormous medicine ball I'm carrying around."

It took only a quick glance to see this Miranda person was pregnant. Very, very pregnant. "Shouldn't you be on medical leave?"

Snapping gum, the FUC agent heaved herself to her feet and held out a hand to Dawn, who eschewed it out of fear of hurting the lopsided woman.

"They tried to keep me home, but I was driving my husband nuts. His name is Chase, by the way. You'll meet him in a minute. He's outside tangling with your giant lizard."

"I heard gunshots. Is Joey dead?"

"Who's Joey?"

"The lizard."

Miranda shrugged. "No idea. I was told to stand

back and let the men handle it. Which, I might add, wouldn't be happening if I could shift into my bunny. I tell you, I can't wait until I get back to myself."

Dawn didn't comment on the fact that a bunny would hardly be a match for the monstrous gecko terrorizing them.

"So, you never told me your name." Miranda cocked her head and waited for an answer.

Dawn froze. A deer caught in questioning headlights.

The agent tapped her chin in thought. "Let me guess. You're Dawn."

Eep! Dawn bolted, only to run into a brick wall. She bounced, but a pair of steady hands caught her before she could fall. One sniff and Dawn whimpered. *Bear.* Oh dear. Could this day get any worse?

Her eyes rose to meet the steady brown stare of the man holding her.

"Miranda, what did you do to scare the doe?" grumbled the really large man.

"Nothing. I just said her name, and she tried to run off. That usually only happens when I unleash my furry menace."

"Well, since your floppy ears aren't showing, I will assume that the deer is one of the fugitives on FUC's wanted list. Am I correct?"

Pinned under his stern gaze, she could only nod. Only a creature with a death wish lied to a bear.

"You don't seem too dangerous. Are you?"

Again, she shook her head.

Miranda snorted. "Don't be so sure, honey bear. I look sweet and innocent too."

"I am well aware appearances can be deceiving, but you are a special case, wife."

"Aw, you say the sweetest things."

Incredulous at the byplay, Dawn couldn't help but ogle back and forth from Miranda's pleased smile to Chase's indulgent one.

She didn't know what to expect next. More strangeness, apparently.

"Unhand my doe!" growled Everett.

"Dough?" Miranda's brows drew together in confusion. "I don't see any money. Are we being robbed? Or do you mean dough as in the pastry kind? I am kind of hungry. Someone ran off before we got to finish our food."

"Not that kind of dough," Everett snapped. "Doe as in a deer, you know, a female deer. The one Chase is holding off the floor."

"You know her?" Chase turned, still holding Dawn dangling.

"Yes."

"You know she's on the wanted list?"

"Yes."

"And yet you didn't turn her in?"

"No."

"Ooh, I smell a juicy story. Anyone got some carrot cake? This is getting interesting." All eyes turned Miranda's way. She shrugged and smiled sheepishly. "What? I wasn't kidding. Me and junior are hungry."

"I just watched you devour a stack of pancakes, a dozen slices of bacon, and four slices of toast." Everett didn't even attempt to hide his awe.

"But I had to skip the fruit-and-cream-filled crepes

to follow the sloth, who said he had to help you with a woodland creature problem at your house. Speaking of which, what happened to the ugly lizard? Did you get him?"

The corners of Everett's lips turned down. "No. He got away."

Dawn slumped. Good thing Chase held on to her still, or she might have dropped into a heap on the floor as her legs went numb. *Joey escaped, and if his words and crazy declarations can be believed, he's going to come back.* Would she never free herself from the nightmare of Mastermind?

"Uh-oh. The deer doesn't look so good. Anyone got a bucket?"

Where a demand to put her down didn't work, the fear of puking did. Chase couldn't thrust her fast enough into Everett's arms. Hugging her tight, he left their impromptu meeting in the hall and headed for the living room, where he sank into a chair with her cradled on his lap.

Miranda and Chase followed, and seconds after a door slam, Tom arrived as well.

"He's gone," Tom announced. "I tried following him, but the bastard can run. And no one told me he was like Spiderman. He jumped onto this building and scaled the thing like he had suction cups for hands and feet."

"Because he does," Dawn volunteered. At the interested glances sent her way, she explained. "Geckos possess special toes with a sticky substance on them that allows them to adhere to most surfaces and climb."

"How cool," Miranda exclaimed, clapping her

hands. "Boy, I'll bet Viktor will be jealous when he finds out."

"Who's Viktor?" Dawn asked.

"My usual partner. He thinks his croc is awesome cool, but he can't scale buildings."

"Yes, it's cool and a pain in the ass," Everett interrupted. "But I don't really care about Joey's abilities right now. I'd rather know what you intend to do about Dawn."

Chase, seated on the couch, leaned forward. "The memo sent out to agents and hired bounty hunters was to apprehend or kill the fugitives on sight."

"Technically, I apprehended," he hedged.

The bear didn't give an inch. He folded his arms over his massive chest. "But you didn't call it in. Care to explain?"

"Oh plllease, honey bear. Even you can see the wolf has the hots for the deer."

"She's a wanted criminal."

"Exactly what I've been telling him," Tom agreed with a nod of his head.

Traitor. See if she made him any more cookies with extra chocolate chips.

Everett jumped to her defense. "Dawn isn't a danger to anyone."

"And how do you know that?"

"Because I do. She's been living with me for days now, and I've yet to see her do anything crazy."

"Well, she did clean your house top to bottom," Tom threw out.

"That's hardly crazy," Chase stated.

"You didn't see it before. Only a madwoman would volunteer to do that."

It occurred to Dawn she should speak in her defense, but the words just wouldn't come. The ordeal with Joey had left her shaken. The current and ongoing encounter with the FUC agents had her trembling. And her position in Everett's lap had her…well, feeling things she shouldn't at the moment, given the gravity of the situation.

"Are you a psychotic murdering monster who likes to eat her victims?"

Dawn gaped at Miranda. Talk about blunt.

"Well?"

"Uh, no."

The pregnant agent smiled widely. "And there you go."

"I hate to rain on your parade, Miranda, but we have orders to bring all of Mastermind's ex-patients in to headquarters."

"Oh, but, honey bear, look at her, shaking like a little wee leaf in the wind. Anyone can see she's harmless."

"At the moment. Who knows what she's like when she turns into her beast." Tom made it sound ominous.

"He's got a point," Chase replied. "I mean, you're a prime example of someone who looks so cute and harmless, yet can turn into the biggest menace known to society."

Miranda beamed. "I see someone's getting some pie later."

For some reason, this made the bear turn an interesting shade of red.

"We're getting off track," Tom pointed out. "We

were talking about Dawn and her refusal to shift. It's obviously because she knows she's dangerous."

"I am not!"

"Says you."

"There's an easy way to solve this," Chase interjected. He fixed his stern gaze on her. "Can you flip into your deer and show us?"

Dawn shook her head. She couldn't keep her shameful secret if she did.

"Why not?"

"Because she's hiding something." Tom announced this with way too much pleasure.

Everett frowned at him. "Why are you so intent on making her out to be a bad guy? She's done nothing to deserve it."

"Other than turn you into someone willing to abet a wanted fugitive. Ever since she arrived on the scene, you haven't been yourself."

"And you're being an ass. Exactly why are you scared of her?"

Scared? Dawn wouldn't have exactly called Tom's dislike of her that, until she happened to glance at him. It struck her in that moment. It wasn't that Tom disliked her—okay, maybe he did a little—but Tom did fear her. Feared she would take his best friend and partner away.

She wanted to reassure him that would never happen. Whatever occurred between her and Everett was temporary. Once the situation with FUC and Joey got resolved, they'd go their separate ways.

Except...it occurred to her she didn't necessarily want to leave. Sure, Everett drove her nuts with his crude language and slovenly behavior, but he was also kind, funny, and caring. He also didn't treat her like an incapable idiot. He trusted her. He wanted her. He… was nuzzling her ear and making it hard to concentrate.

"Would you stop that?" she hissed.

"Sorry. My wolf isn't happy that you're smelling so funny."

"Well, rubbing yourself all over me isn't going to make things better." Unless they were naked.

A thought he echoed as he nibbled on her neck. "I wouldn't be so sure of that."

"Do you need a moment to yourselves?" Miranda asked. "Considering how many times I've dragged Chase into a private corner for some *us* time, I'm sure we can spare you a few minutes if it will help."

Cheeks burning, Dawn hopped off Everett's lap. "Nope. I'm fine, thank you. Everett and I aren't involved in that way."

"Not for lack of trying," the jerk added.

"Sure you aren't." Miranda winked at her.

"Can we focus back on the task at hand?" Chase rumbled. "We have a murderous gecko on the loose, one that needs apprehension."

"What about Dawn?"

"For the moment, she seems like the least of our problems. So we'll hold off on doing anything, but I will have to report her presence. The fact she's aiding in our investigation and ongoing quest to track the killer should help her case."

"Speaking of tracking, what was the lizard doing here?" Bubbly Miranda disappeared and a keen-eyed agent took her place.

Dawn, who'd taken up pacing behind the couch, sighed. "Apparently, he was after me."

"He wanted to make you into deer stew?"

"Not quite. More like his deer-ly beloved." At their stares, Dawn explained. "It seems Joey has had a crush on me since our days of incarceration. He's got it in his pea-sized brain that we're meant to be together. He thinks Everett is holding me against my will and came to rescue me."

"He's insane," Everett barked.

"Way to point out the obvious," Tom remarked dryly.

"How can we use this to our advantage?" Miranda mused.

Everett bristled. "Excuse me? What do you mean advantage? We are not using Dawn as bait in any scheme."

"Why ever not?" Miranda asked.

"Because," Everett sputtered, "it's dangerous."

"Well duh." The bunny agent rolled her eyes. "He's a killer, but at the same time, how else do you expect to get him to come out of hiding again?"

"Much as I hate to say it, my wife has a point. We need something to draw the gecko out. If he's got an attachment to Dawn, we should use that."

"She could get hurt."

"And people could die if we don't," Tom said.

"I'll do it." Dawn couldn't believe she'd spoken the words. Bravery wasn't her strong suit, but she had to do something, not just to save any poor souls Joey might come across, but for her own peace of mind. Knowing Joey was out there, waiting for a chance to get his claws on her again… She'd do whatever it took to get him into custody. "Besides, I have a bear, a sloth, and the big, bad wolf on my side."

"And while I might not be able to turn into my bunny, I'm an excellent shot," Miranda boasted.

With a team like that at her back, what could go wrong? She refused to pay any attention to the list her mind came up with.

18

So many things could go wrong. That was all Everett could think of once they finally broke up their gathering hours later after hashing out plan after plan to use Dawn as bait and lure Joey into a trap.

He tried to divert them from their path, not at all comfortable with the idea of placing Dawn in danger. His delicate doe wasn't cut out for the possible violence that might erupt. He'd been outvoted, even by Dawn, who seemed determined to prove to FUC that she was on their side.

Once the FUC agents left for their hotel with promises to return early in the morning, Everett waited only long enough for Tom's snores to begin before he snuck into his bedroom. Or he meant to. When he turned the knob and pushed, the door wouldn't budge. He shoved harder, but something blocked it. Dawn had barricaded the entrance!

"Open this door right now," he hissed, knowing she

wasn't asleep. He could hear her breathing just on the other side of the flimsy portal.

"Or what? You'll huff and puff and blow the door down?"

"And make my to-do list of repairs longer? Not a chance."

"Then I guess you're sleeping with snoring beauty."

"This isn't funny, Dawn."

"Why do you want in?"

"We need to talk."

"I think we've talked enough. I'm all talked out. You are not changing my mind. I am going to help bring Joey down."

"But—"

"No buts, Everett. I am not going to live my life running and hiding. Not anymore. The only way to set myself free is to capture Joey and clear my name with FUC."

"I don't like it." He slumped against the door and slid down until he sat on the floor.

"So you've expressed, quite loudly and often. What I don't get is why. Why do you care what happens to me?"

Why did he? Sure they'd flirted. He found her attractive and vice versa. She liked cooking; he liked eating the results. He dirtied; she cleaned. She talked; he listened. He found her interesting. Her smile lit up a room. Her scent drove him wild. Her absence made him anxious. Her safety was of utmost important. Her happiness was the only thing that mattered. He loved her.

What. The. Hell.

DOE AND THE WOLF

He slapped himself in the head and ran through the reasons why he cared for Dawn, and once again, the big L word popped up.

Oh crap. When had that happened? How had he gone from carefree bachelor trying to get in her pants to being a wolf on the prowl intent on being the only one in her pants?

"Even you don't know why." She sighed, not realizing the epiphany of epic proportions taking place in his head and heart. "Just think, once we get rid of Joey, you can go back to normal. I'll leave. Tom will go home, and you'll have your life back. You'll be free to return to your slobby ways and womanizing." She said the last bit in a sad tone, which made his ears perk. Did she want to stay? Had she come to care for him too?

"It hasn't been all bad having you around."

She snorted. "Sure it hasn't. I've stolen your bedroom, your best friend is sleeping on the couch, and you had a giant lizard in here today wrecking the joint."

"Hazards of the job."

"One that will disappear once we catch Joey and I leave."

"Where will you go?"

He could almost hear her shrug. "I don't know. I might go back to the woods for a bit and stay at the cabin until I find a job."

That ramshackle hut in the middle of nowhere? "Winter is coming. That place isn't going to provide much shelter once the cold starts."

"It's not like I have much of a choice. Once I get some money aside, I'll find a place in town."

"What did you used to do before?"

"I was a receptionist for a dentist."

He saw an opening and dove on it. "You know, I could use someone to answer phones and stuff."

"I didn't realize you were that busy."

"I'm not," he admitted. "But that wouldn't be all. You could take care of paperwork and keeping the office running."

"You mean your garage?"

"Hey, it has a desk and a filing cabinet."

Her soft chuckled warmed him. "You are something else, wolf."

"So is that a yes?"

"I don't know if it's a good idea. Actually, I know it isn't."

"Why?"

"It just isn't."

He said aloud what she couldn't. "Because we're attracted to each other."

"That's part of it."

At least she didn't deny it. "Is that such a bad thing?"

"Depends. What happens if we can't keep it professional?"

"I'm hoping we don't. I want you, little doe."

"That's all well and good, but what about when you don't? Then what happens to me?"

"I won't let you down."

Silence.

"Dawn?"

"You make it sound so tempting," she replied softly.

"Would it help if I said I've never felt about another woman like I do with you?"

"Oh please."

"I'm serious. I won't deny I'm usually a make 'em howl and leave 'em kind of guy, but with you, it's different. I don't just want to have sex with you."

"Says the guy who hasn't stopped trying since we met."

"Hey, you're hot, what else do you expect? But seriously. You make me want things, Dawn. I like having you here in my house."

"Because you have clean clothes and hot meals."

"It's more than that, and you know it. I have fun with you."

"So do I."

The admission made his heart swell. "Do you know you're the first woman I've ever really talked to? Connected with? Getting to know you and spending time with you has been awesome. I want more. Don't you?"

Silence again.

Way to stab his ego. He wondered if by being honest he'd scared her off. Good news was he didn't hear the window opening, which meant she hadn't escaped. Bad news, though, she didn't reply.

Furniture scraped as it was pulled to the side. The door swung open, and Everett, who leaned against it, flopped onto his back and grinned up at her.

"Hey, little doe. You'll be glad to know from this angle, I don't spot any hairs on your chinny chin chin."

19

Dawn couldn't help but laugh and shake her head at him. How could she not? Despite the fact he was a wolf, a known womanizer and a bad boy, she couldn't resist him, not when he said all the right things. Not when she feared what tomorrow might bring.

Who knew what the future held? Would she survive the Joey fiasco? Would FUC let her remain free? Did Everett care for her as he claimed, or was this another ploy to get in her pants?

She didn't have any answers, but she did know one thing. *Time to stop running.* Not just from the danger Mastermind had created before her death, but also from her own feelings. She wanted Everett. Wanted him as a lover. Wanted the future he proposed. She just plain wanted to live, love, and not worry about tomorrow.

Regret was something she could deal with later, but she'd rather regret letting him into her heart than always wonder if she'd let slip free the chance for something great.

DOE AND THE WOLF

She crouched over him. "You know, for a guy who doesn't want to be compared to the wolf in stories, you use an awful lot of quotes. And, for future reference, telling a woman she doesn't have hair on her chin is not a great way to convince her to become your lover."

"Maybe not. Let me try again then." His hand cupped her head and pulled her down. She flattened her palms on either side of his head to steady herself but didn't stop the descent of her mouth toward his. Their lips touched. Awareness sizzled. Her breath rushed out in a soft exhalation, which he took in before he took her mouth and claimed it for his own.

Ever felt like something was missing in life? That a puzzle piece needed to complete the picture had gone astray? Kissing Everett was that "Aha!" moment, where the thing she'd been looking for fell into place. Suddenly, she couldn't remember why this was a bad idea, or why she'd wanted to fight their attraction in the first place.

Kissing him was the most natural, wonderful, and right thing in the world. And she couldn't get enough. How they made it to the bed, she couldn't have said. One moment they necked on the floor, the next they lay on the mattress, their clothing having been discarded along the way, leaving them skin to skin. And what skin he had.

The flesh on his back might prove smooth, but his chest... Furry curls tickled her bare breasts, the friction making her giggle.

"I'm almost afraid to ask why you're laughing," he said in between nibbles of her earlobe.

"I was just thinking about how you compared your chest to a rug. It is."

"Don't tell me you're surprised. You saw it enough times."

"Seeing it and feeling it are two different things. Before, I was still clothed, but now—" She wiggled atop him, the springy hair dragging across her feverish, sensitized skin. "Now I get to enjoy it."

He groaned as she went on her own exploration of his body, her teeth nipping at his neck, her body slowly gliding down the length of his, not far, because the hardness of his shaft projected between her thighs and pressed against her core. The feel of him, so close, sent a shudder through her, and moisture pooled in her sex.

She wasn't ready to stop yet, though, and give in, no matter how her body clamored for her to climb atop. She kissed his flat nipples, licking them as he writhed.

"Damn it, Dawn," he growled. "I'm supposed to be the one seducing you."

She laughed. "Keep protesting and I won't tell you what a big cock you have, all the better to—"

He dragged her up so his lips could mash against hers, a fiery kiss that stole her breath, and all thoughts of teasing fled her mind. All thought left except one. *I need him.*

Raising her hips, she positioned herself over him, the head of his shaft bobbing and searching for the warm haven of her pussy. It didn't take much maneuvering to get him where she wanted him, his fat head sliding between her moist lips. She sat down on him, sheathing him in a fell swoop that drew a hoarse cry as his fingers dug into her buttocks.

DOE AND THE WOLF

Aah. How right he felt inside her, his thickness stretching the pulsing walls of her channel. She rocked, driving him deeper, grinding her clit against him. A shudder went through his body, and she couldn't help a spasm in her sex, one that clenched him tight.

He groaned aloud then panted. "You're going to drive me wild, little doe."

"Seems only right given we're both animals at heart," she murmured back, rocking again. Her breath caught as he swelled even thicker within her. Mmm, the pressure felt good. She raked her fingernails down his chest as she sat up on him, a wiggle driving him even deeper inside. Head thrown back, she rode him, bouncing and grinding while his hands on her waist guided her into a rhythm.

Blissful pleasure built, coiled, tightened all her muscles until she thought she'd burst.

She came in a glorious wave of ecstasy, her sex shuddering and gripping and undulating while he thrust and yelled and pushed.

For a moment, she drifted, glowing with the aftermath. Breathing heavily, she collapsed on his chest and listened to his frantically beating heart.

"Damn, Dawn."

"Is that a good damn?"

"What do you think?" he whispered, kissing her forehead, cheeks, and then her lips. "If I had the strength to howl, I would."

"Does this mean you're done for the night?"

He stiffened underneath her, and she didn't mean just his dignity.

Thankfully, he found the stamina to go again, and

this time, they both howled—which set the neighborhood dogs barking, but curled in his arms, a smile on her lips, Dawn didn't care.

Her wolf would protect her from the predators.

But who will save me from the wolf?

20

WAKING up snuggled with the woman he loved made Everett smile, a grin he couldn't wipe from his face as he let Dawn sleep and left her—lest he maul her delectable body again—and made himself a coffee. A tousled-haired Tom, who stumbled into the kitchen with one eye open, couldn't help but notice.

"I see you finally tickled the doe. Looks like you enjoyed it."

"A gentleman never tells."

"I wasn't aware you knew any."

Even Tom's cranky mood couldn't bring Everett down from his high. "Maybe it just took the right woman to show me the light."

"Or she infected you with her madness."

"If this is how it feels to be insane, then you don't know what you're missing."

"You are way too happy for a guy who's about to put his ladyfriend in the path of a psychotic killer."

Tom finally hit the mark, and Everett's good humor

sank faster than his favorite lure when his brother had tossed it in the pond when they were kids. He grumbled, "Way to remind me."

"Someone has to keep you grounded. You seem to be getting way too attached to this girl."

"And? What's the problem with that?"

"The fact that when we catch this lizard, she's going to jail."

"Maybe. From what I gleaned, the bigheads on the shifter council only wanted to capture her if she proved a menace because of the experimentation. I think it's pretty obvious by now that Dawn's not dangerous." Apparently, a few other shifters had been granted clemency, Viktor's foxy girlfriend, Renee, being one of them.

"Not dangerous? Really? How do you know that for sure? Have you seen her animal?"

Everett's one hazy recollection wasn't quite clear and couldn't be accurate. He shook his head.

"Then, for all we know, she turns into a rampaging psycho, murdering deer."

"You forgot the part where I drool acid and my eyes turn red and shoot out laser beams," Dawn mocked as she strode into the kitchen, barefoot and wearing one of Everett's shirts, which hung to her knees. She looked good enough to *eat. Awooo!*

"Hardy-har-har, Bambi. If you're so damned harmless, why won't you show us your animal?"

Dawn took a sip of her coffee before answering. "Because I don't want to."

"Because you're a mutant, just like Joey."

"Different than I used to be, yes, but nothing like that crazy lizard."

"And we're supposed to take your word for it?" Tom fired back.

"I don't care what you do. I haven't seen your sloth, and you don't see me accusing you of being some monster."

"Because I'm normal."

"Are you sure? Because the way you snore, I'd say there is something definitely wrong with you."

Tom's red face and the bulging vein in his forehead didn't bode well. Everett jumped in to calm matters. "Stop it, you two. We have more important things to do today than bicker."

"He started it," she muttered.

"One phone call from me and I can finish it," Tom threatened.

"Enough!" Everett snapped. "Tom, stop threatening Dawn." She stuck her tongue out at the sloth. "Dawn, stop baiting Tom." Tom smirked back.

As for Everett? He closed his eyes and wished he was dealing with pigs again.

He couldn't understand Tom's hostility. Why was he so determined to hate Dawn? She'd done nothing to deserve the level of animosity aimed her way. Teasing aside, she'd done Tom no injury and proven an asset to have around.

Given his attitude, how am I going to tell him I hired her and asked her to stay once the case is over? Paint his belly yellow, but Everett didn't want to cross that bridge anytime soon. He was used to being the cause of trouble, not the referee breaking it up.

How could he make Tom see Dawn wasn't a danger? It would help if Dawn would show them her deer. Even Everett couldn't deny that her adamant refusal to change shapes was odd. He wished he could remember with more clarity his time at the river when she'd saved him. His fuzzy recollection implied there was something off about her shape, but he just couldn't pinpoint what.

But, so long as he didn't wake to her gnawing on him, with less than erotic intent, he'd have to trust his instinct, which said Dawn wouldn't hurt a mouse.

An uneasy truce called, he and Dawn headed for a shower—and he hoped a quickie—before they started their day and took their first stab at coaxing Joey out of hiding and into custody.

Last night's lovemaking had proved glorious. Dawn, while seeming prim and proper when it came to sex outside the bedroom, became a veritable wild woman behind closed doors. She gave entirely of herself when it came to passion.

When she'd spoken dirty to him the night before, damn, he'd just about shot his load in surprise. She more than surpassed his needs and expectations in a lover, making his discovery of his feelings for her even more intense now that he knew how compatible they were, not just outside the bedroom but in it.

It made him eager for another taste, although she initially tried to forestall him. When she entered the bathroom, he was right on her heels. She whirled and stopped him in his tracks with a hand on his chest.

"What are doing?"

"Taking a shower."

"Not right now you aren't. I'm going first," she declared. "It takes me longer to dry my hair than you."

"Who says we're taking turns? I say we conserve time and water and shower together."

A snort escaped her. "Oh please. We both know that's the corniest excuse ever. You just want to have sex."

"Yup."

"Too bad. Not happening."

He put on his best puppy face. "Why not?"

"Because Tom is out there waiting for his turn."

"He might be my best friend, but I draw the line at him having sex with you."

Her jaw dropped and she squeaked, "What? I didn't mean that kind of turn. I meant he was waiting to get in the shower."

Everett laughed. "I know. I just wanted to see the look on your face. Don't worry about Tom. He can use the shower in the basement. I've got on-demand hot water units in both bathrooms. We can take as long as we want."

"We need to stay focused on what we have to do today."

"How am I supposed to concentrate when all I can think of is how yummy you look this morning and how much I want to bend you over and—"

She blushed as she slapped a hand over his mouth. "Don't say it."

He arched a brow before prying her fingers loose. "After last night, you cannot convince me you're a prude. I heard the words that came out of that delightfully dirty mouth of yours, little doe."

"That was in the heat of the moment."

"A moment we're about to enjoy again. So stop arguing. You won't win."

When she tried to protest, he hummed the most annoying tune he could think of and turned on the shower. When she would have left, he slid himself in front of the door and dropped his pants. That got her attention. It also brought the right kind of flush to her cheeks, the heated kind that was also reflected in her gaze.

Her tongue flicked out and licked her lower lip. "I guess if we made it quick…"

Seeing an opening, he dove on it. With deft hands, he stripped her shirt and panties before carting her into the shower stall. Keeping her mouth busy, and full, his tongue plying it with sensual caresses, he let his hands explore her body with a bar of soap. Lathering her with suds was a great way to both clean and play with her delightful body. Under his caresses, her nipples pebbled with awareness and need. He flicked his thumbs over the peaks, stroking them and loving how she sighed into his mouth and her hips arched forward, seeking contact with his body.

Pressing her against the glass tile wall, he bracketed hands on either side of her head and leaned into her, enough to let his erection poke at the junction of her thighs. She trapped it between her legs and let her hips rock, dragging him back and forth against her sex.

He sucked in a breath. "Damn, Dawn."

"Like that?"

"Yeah. Too much."

She uttered a soft laugh as she continued to tease.

"If you don't stop, this is going to be quicker than we'd both like."

"I don't mind quick." She cupped his face and pressed kisses to his lips, jaw, anywhere she could reach. "Take me, Everett. I need you."

Oh and how he wanted her too. But, first, he needed a taste. Angling her under the spray, he rinsed the soap from her silky skin before he went to his knees in worship, putting his face level with her pussy.

She didn't protest. On the contrary, her fingers clasped his wet strands, her legs parted, and she lifted one foot to plant it on the bench in his shower, exposing herself to him.

Oh full freaking moon, she was gorgeous. And perfect. And...*tasty*.

No one could resist an offering like that. He nuzzled her, loving how she trembled in expectation; however, teasing only tortured them both. He couldn't hold back from what he truly wanted to do.

His tongue lapped at her sex, licking her from her sensitive clit across her juicy lips right to the crevice of her buttocks. She keened and undulated as he pleasured her, her hips writhing in delight, her pants and cries the music that guided his actions.

As she approached her peak, he debated having her come on his tongue, feeling the quiver of her orgasm against his mouth, but he was a selfish wolf. He wanted to spoil himself and feel her ultimate release. Bask in her pleasure as she pulsed around his cock and screamed in his ear.

He rose, spinning her as he did so she faced away and presented the smooth line of her back and the rounded curve of her ass. She sensed what he wanted and placed her palms flat against the wall, thrusting her buttocks out in invitation.

Wanting to take a bit of control from his demanding doe, he kicked her feet farther apart and reached a hand between her thighs to rub a rough finger against her clit. She moaned, the wetness of her core a slippery heat that begged for him.

He grabbed his cock one-handed and slapped it against her. She squeaked. He slapped it again, and she shuddered.

Between her plump lips he inserted it, the tightness of her almost too much to bear. In he wiggled and pushed, the tightness of her channel, plus the water from the shower removing her natural lube, making it a snug fit. A less experienced wolf might have lost it then. He instead let loose a partial howl and breathed through his nose as he sat partially wedged, holding back, waiting for her to adjust.

She had no such patience.

She rammed herself back and took him deeper. So much for control. His snapped. He knew he wouldn't be long, not with her pulsing and squeezing and making every thrust and stroke so deliciously pleasurable. He reached around to the front of her mound, his fingers finding and rubbing her clit as he pounded into her welcoming sheath.

In the warm steam and persistent rain flow of his shower, they undulated and rode the wave to bliss, his shout of culmination followed almost immediately by her scream of orgasm. The muscles of her sex milked him, wrung him out to dry, took everything he had, and gave him back ecstasy in spades.

Overcome with sensation, he curved his body into hers, his hips still jerking, even though he'd come. He was intent on drawing out her bliss. A primal urge came over him as he licked and nibbled the skin at her nape. He bit her, not hard enough to break skin, but enough to leave a bruising mark.

She came again with a scream to shatter glass, and just about ripped his cock off, so strongly did it echo through her body.

Way to make a wolf proud.

His second howl could probably be heard around the world. *A-fucking-wooo!*

21

So they didn't save water or time, but they definitely got clean, eventually. Not to mention sated.

By the time Dawn left that bathroom on wobbly legs and prune-wrinkled feet, she had almost forgotten the dangerous task ahead of her.

She remembered really quickly. Sobered by her upcoming role to play, she dressed in silence, and Everett, for once, didn't try to tease her out of it. He did, however, take every opportunity to touch her, a brush of his hand across her nape, a kiss to her temple, a hug. Small amorous gestures that bolstered her.

And kept her from fleeing as instinct demanded.

As plans went, the one they'd come up with the previous day didn't please everybody, least of all Everett, but it was all they could devise. Everett's biggest problem with it was the fact Dawn was about to get dangled, similar to a worm on a hook, to draw in Joey.

The plan was simple. Given Joey's ability to climb,

he could be anywhere in the neighborhood and, with his aerial vantage point, spot Everett or the others well before they could track him down and corner him. So they had to lure him out of hiding. Give him a reason to hit the ground where he could be nabbed or taken out. Hence the mock fight.

Or not so mock fight.

Emerging from the bedroom, and before the shower, Dawn couldn't help but notice the tense atmosphere between Everett and Tom. It hung in the air, a miasma of discord with one cause. Her.

It was obvious Tom guessed what had transpired between them the night before and heartily disapproved. It irked Dawn that he disliked her so much; after all, she'd done him no harm. Not that it mattered, hence her constant verbal teasing of him and sassy remarks, which probably didn't help the situation.

Usually, she wouldn't have cared. After all, what did one person's opinion matter? However, given her relationship with Everett, she couldn't avoid Tom, not to mention she hated being the reason the two best friends were at odds. She just didn't know how to fix it, short of leaving permanently.

But Everett didn't want to let her go, and if she was honest, she didn't want to leave. Something Tom found out after their shower when the wolf told his partner of his plan to hire Dawn, and that's when things exploded verbally.

"Hire her? Are you out of your furry mind?" Tom bellowed. "She's a criminal."

"Who did no crime but be in the wrong place at the

wrong time. Or are you too blind to see she's a victim in all this?"

"You're not thinking with the right head," Tom retorted.

"There is nothing wrong with either of them. I don't understand what your problem is. Dawn's been nothing but nice and helpful."

"So you're going to hire a known criminal because she's a good screw? I never knew sex was a requirement for the job."

"I won't have you insult her." Everett's fist hung clenched at his side and his jaw angled in an angry way that didn't bode well.

"Where's the insult? It's true. Ever since you met her, you've been panting after her ass. I'd hoped once you tapped it, you'd come to your senses."

"Why can't you accept the fact that Dawn is special?"

"Oh, she's special all right. So special I'll probably be writing your obituary when you let your guard down and she shows her true colors."

"Enough!" Everett slammed a fist on the kitchen counter, while Dawn could only sit on a chair, a silent spectator, who didn't have the guts to stand in the middle of a fight that had brewed between the guys since she'd come on the scene. "Doe is staying, and that's final."

"You're making a mistake," Tom snapped before slamming out of the house.

"Maybe he's right. Maybe this is a bad idea." Dawn picked at the seam of her jeans, her earlier euphoria faded in the face of Tom's continued dislike and distrust.

"What is? Working for me or sleeping with me?"

"Both." She tried to ignore the hurt on his face. It couldn't hurt worse than her heart. *You should have known better than to think you could have happily-ever-after with a wolf,* she could almost hear her mother say.

"How can you say that after everything I told you? Or are you saying my feelings don't matter?"

"Of course they do, it's just you shouldn't be fighting with Tom. He's your best friend."

"And you're my lover."

The word hung in the air between them.

Lover.

Not one-night-stand. Not secretary. Or fuck buddy.

Lover implied something deeper, with emotional connection.

She let out a frustrated cry. "Everything is so complicated."

"The best things in life aren't easy. My da always used to say the things you appreciate most are the things you fight for. Of course, he said that mostly after he went hunting and brought back some big game for the family to eat, but in this case, I think the expression works."

The plastic thing in her ear crackled before she could reply.

"It's time. Chase thinks he spotted the lizard a few houses down on a rooftop," Miranda said.

She didn't need to tell Everett. He'd heard. "Time for me to get some air."

"We're not done talking about this, Dawn."

She knew they weren't, which was what made their mock fight easier to fake. The frustration was very real, as was the turmoil in her mind.

"I don't belong with you. We're opposites."

"You know what they say, little doe, opposites attract."

"Or kill each other."

"I'd never hurt you."

"Wasn't that what your ancestor said to the girl in the red hood?"

"Great granddad was a ruffian. And this isn't a fairy tale."

"No. It's not. Welcome to the modern day. And who says I'm worried about you killing me. Maybe I was talking about myself."

He snorted.

"Don't laugh. According to Tom, I'm dangerous."

"And according to Tom, so are chick flicks, Doritos, and the use of cellphones."

Why was he so determined to convince her? Why couldn't he see the obvious? "We come from two different species. Everyone knows predators and prey shouldn't mix."

"Has anyone told that to Miranda and Chase?"

"They're a special case."

"I know you care for me."

She did, enough that she had to wonder if the right thing was to walk away.

"Um, I hate to interrupt an obviously personal moment," Miranda interjected via her earpiece, "but you need to kick this fight up a notch and take it public if you want to make it believable."

Dawn opened the front door and stepped out onto the concrete porch, Everett at her heels. "I won't let you leave me, Dawn."

"I am not yours to command, and you can't make me stay!" she yelled as she marched down the steps.

"Get back here, Dawn." Everett hollered back. "We're not done talking."

"Oh yes we are. And don't you dare follow or I'll sic the cops on you. I need some space."

"If you get in trouble, don't you dare call me, because I won't answer."

"Fine."

"Fine." He slammed the door.

Off she strode, hands in her pockets, head ducked as if in thought, and part of her was wondering what to do about Tom, Everett, and the situation she found herself in. But the other part of her remained very much aware that Joey probably lurked. A knot in her gut, instinct, screamed he'd been spying.

And hopefully had fallen for the bait.

Shaking on the inside, their fake fight necessary in case Joey watched but leaving her feeling sick to her stomach because she loathed subterfuge, she practically trotted along the sidewalk, eyes and ears open to the sound of a follower. Despite knowing the FUC agents were already in position, along with Tom keeping an eye on her, she wasn't completely reassured. In order to make Joey believe Dawn was on her own, Everett needed to stay put for the moment—the part of the plot he liked least and the aspect he'd argued most vehemently about.

"I don't want to stay behind. It's too dangerous."

"*Only until we know Joey's taken the bait and isn't watching you or the house,*" Chase explained. "*He needs to think Dawn's alone and vulnerable.*"

"*It makes her an easy target.*"

"*She won't ever be out of our sight. I'll be in the van watching and listening from the camera we're going to have pinned to her jacket,*" Miranda said.

"*That won't keep her from harm if Joey decides to attack her instead of trying to kidnap her,*" Everett growled.

In the end, Everett got outvoted. Joey wouldn't come out of hiding if he thought for a moment the wolf was nearby. So, they had their fake fight, Dawn stomped off and prayed nothing went wrong. Despite all their reassurances they'd be close by, Dawn couldn't help but hunch her shoulders as the prickly sensation of being watched creeped her out. She might not have a super-duper nose like Everett, but the woodland creature in her sensed danger nearby. Joey was watching.

The neighborhood, which sported a mix of suburban housing, low-rise complexes, and town houses, was quiet this time of the day. Mid-morning and mid-week, most people were at work, so the sidewalks were mostly empty, and only the occasional car whizzed by. Dawn's footsteps slapped the concrete sidewalk in a steady rhythm as she tread block after block away from Everett, the distance increasing her angst.

Ahead, parked along the side of the road, right in front of a mini strip mall boasting a corner store, drycleaner, and Chinese takeout restaurant, she spotted the utility van Miranda hid in with the surveillance equipment. Despite Miranda's boast of being an excellent marksman, the guys deemed the bunny too pregnant to participate in the takedown. But Miranda didn't give in without a fight.

"Honey bear, you're tempting me to cut off your supply of pie."

"I'm doing this for your own good," Chase snarled back, arms crossed over his chest, an implacable mountain in the face of her perky fury.

In the end, cute threats and too many references to pie later, he won. And Dawn learned a whole bunch of new eye-opening insults.

The FUC duo was a mismatched couple. How she would dearly love to know how a bunny and a bear got together and somehow made it work. Did it mean a pairing between Everett and Dawn could as well, minus the pie?

Everett was right. Opposites did attract, and despite her fear, a part of her desperately wanted to try. If she did, though, she'd have to divulge her secret. Could Everett handle it? She barely could. She knew her family wouldn't if they knew what Mastermind had done to her doe.

But maybe the fact he's not one to conform will make him more accepting. There was only one way to find out. She'd have to bite the bullet and reveal herself to him. Either he'd accept her for who she now was, or he wouldn't. Only one way to find out. She'd have to shift, and in front of an audience so that maybe at the same time she could finally allay Tom's fears. Or reinforce them.

The big revelation would have to wait, though. First, she needed to help capture her unwanted suitor.

She strolled along, a ball of anxiety roiling in her

tummy as she waited for Joey to make his move. She went several blocks, past the panel van with the watching Miranda, past the bushes and shadowy crevices between homes and low-rise apartments. She was ready for Joey to leap out at her, eye twitching, blubbering his inane claims of affection.

She reached the intersection with traffic lights and stopped. He'd not made his move. She pursed her lips. They'd hoped Joey would make his presence known before she reached this busy area. Less chance of their actions getting noticed by humans.

But he'd foiled that plan. So there was only one thing to do—return the way she came with an even slower step and hope Joey fell for it this time.

As she drew even with the van, the logo Critter Exterminators Inc. painted on the side, the panel in the side slid open, and she turned her head to ask Miranda if she'd seen anything. The bunny had. As a matter of fact, Miranda was entertaining Joey, who held a gun against her large belly.

"Get in, or we'll be having bunny stew," Joey declared with all too much glee.

What the heck had gone wrong? With no choice, Dawn clambered in.

The door slammed shut, and Joey motioned her into the driver's seat, all the while keeping his gun trained on the pregnant belly of one seriously annoyed Miranda.

"My dearest Dawn. So glad you could join us."

"I don't think you left me much of a choice."

"I thought having a chat with your friend might get your attention."

"You have my undivided attention. What do you want?"

"Here's what's going to happen," Joey stated in a low, monotone voice. "You're going to pull out and, obeying the rules of the road, drive us to the national park. You're going to do so without attracting attention, or else."

"Else what?" Miranda asked, followed by a loud snap of her chewing gum.

"Or else the rabbit gets it!"

"No need for violence," Dawn replied in a soothing tone, trying to keep him calm.

It might have worked if Miranda was on the same wavelength. "Hey, is it true you can lick your own eyeball?" Miranda asked in all seriousness. Dawn could not decide what was more shocking—a serious Miranda or the oddball question.

Joey gritted his teeth and proved his bulging eyeballs could both tic at the same time. "I am not warning you again, rabbit. Keep your mouth shut, or you and the bun in the oven will be saying bye-bye."

"You know, all these threats to me and the baby, not to mention the whole kidnapping thing, are really going to piss my husband off," Miranda claimed. "Chase might seem like a soft and cuddly grizzly, but he's a real bear where I'm concerned."

"I'm not worried about your partner. I'm more than a match for Yogi."

Miranda winced. "Ooh. He hates that nickname."

"I don't care. Soon, he and the rest of FUC gang will be filling my belly. I'm stronger than anything they can throw at me."

"And I thought Mastermind was nuts," Miranda muttered.

"Don't call me that!" Joey yelled. He pushed the barrel of the gun against the bulging midsection of the FUC agent, who could have really used a duct tape gag. The tic under Joey's eyes pulsed faster and faster.

Uh-oh. Dawn was starting to realize the rapidity of the muscle spasm was the precursor to trouble.

"You'll have to excuse her, Joey. Pregnancy hormones, you know, they make women a little nuts." Dawn twirled a finger beside her head and pasted a weak smile on her lips. "She's going to behave. We both are, aren't we, Miranda?" Dawn stressed with a pointed glare in the bunny's direction.

"Some people are no fun." Miranda sulked in her seat, but clamped her lips tight.

The twitch eased. "That's more like it. What are you waiting for, my beloved doe? Get us out of here."

With no other choice, Dawn squeezed into the driver's seat and eased the panel van out onto the road. She waited until they'd driven a few blocks before asking, "Mind if I ask how you and Joey got acquainted?"

"I had to pee," Miranda admitted, her tone embarrassed. "When I got back to the van, he was waiting inside, masked under the smell of a bag of freshly baked carrot muffins."

"You didn't find it odd someone left muffins in the truck?" Dawn couldn't help but query.

Miranda shrugged. "Chase is very considerate that way. So no. I didn't find it strange. But don't worry, despite what fly breath here thinks, Chase and the boys will find us and rescue us. Or at least distract our lizard friend here long enough for me to take care of business."

Dawn almost mimicked Joey's snort. Given the sweat beading Miranda's upper lip, the way her eyes dilated, and her nose scrunched every two minutes, Dawn, who'd seen a fair number of her aunts go into labor over the years, suspected the only thing Miranda would take care of was birthing the babe in her belly.

Dawn wanted to bounce her forehead off the steering wheel in frustration. In all their planning, the bunny going pee or giving birth while trying to apprehend Joey had never made it into any of their scenarios.

Everett was going to freak when he found out she'd gone missing. As for Chase…they all heard the roar of rage even from a few blocks away, and a peek in the rearview mirror showed a rare sight. It wasn't every day you saw a grizzly running down the street chasing traffic.

But even a predator such as a bear couldn't outrace a gas vehicle. It wasn't long before they were out of sight.

And hope, because Dawn wasn't stupid. Miranda was in no shape to fight, and as for Dawn, well, what could her doe do against a raging lunatic gecko?

Eep!

22

"What do you mean they're gone?" Everett practically huffed the words. "What happened to this plan is foolproof?"

"It was—"

"—Not!" Chase roared at Tom. The grizzly was not at all happy his wife was in the slimy hands of the gecko.

Tom pursed his lips. "How were any of us to know Joey would use the manhole the van was parked over to sneak into it while your wife went to pee?"

"Instead of assigning blame, why don't we figure out where they've gone?" Everett was getting mighty tired of his new role as pacifier. When would things revert back to normal where he was the idiot out of control with everyone else trying to keep him out of trouble?

"How are we supposed to locate them?" Chase growled. "It's not like the lizard left a map or a note."

"They're in an FUC van. Call head office and get

them to pull the GPS coordinates on it." What a scary day when a wolf was the voice of reason.

Yanking out his cell phone, Chase dialed the tech department. Sheepish expressions abounded and thumbs twiddled as Chase, his brow furrowed, muttered the occasional, "Yup. Uh-huh. Gotcha."

When he hung up, he held out his device, and they could all see the map with the flashing red icon. "We've got them. They're heading to the park the gecko was recently using for his home base."

"Interesting choice," Everett mused.

"Not really. He's obviously itching for a showdown." Tom cocked his hands into two guns and mimed a cowboy style shooting.

"Oh, he's going to get one all right," Chase rumbled. "And by the time I'm done with him, he'll wish he'd never been born."

"I second that!" Finally, something Everett could approve of. Violence and a takedown.

As for Tom, he didn't add to the bloodthirsty boasts, but the sloth did yell, "Shotgun!"

Jerk.

23

Things I never want to do again. Top of her list, stumbling through the woods, accompanied by a pregnant bunny clutching her belly and yelling "Ow!" every two minutes. Second on her list was being followed by a twitching gecko, sporting an impressive tin foil hat, prodding them with a gun. What a difference from the last time she'd strolled through these parts.

Couldn't she rewind the clock and return to Everett's bed, where the only thing she worried about was the chafe marks on her thighs from his sideburns as he pleasured her?

Thinking of the wolf made her sigh. If she got out of this mess, was there a future for them? Could he truly reform his maverick wolf ways? Did she dare trust him, not just with her heart, but with the fact she wasn't normal like other shifter girls? She wanted to. Wanted to believe they could have a future together. She loved the hairy canine, even if he burped at the table and left his socks on the floor.

Loved him. Wow. It was probably the first time she'd freely admitted that, even if only in her head. She loved the wolf. She didn't care about their differences. Didn't care if her parents wouldn't approve, or that his family might put on some bibs and pull out the carving knife if they met her. *I love Everett.* But was love enough? She'd never know if she didn't give it a try. And who cared what anyone else thought?

As for Tom, he'd have to get over his issues with her. In time, he'd see that Everett was still his friend, albeit one with a steady woman in his life. Speaking of which, maybe they could set Tom up with a ladyfriend of his own. If he had less time on his hands to spend at Everett's, then he wouldn't be so worried about who Everett chose to spend his off-time with. If that failed, there were always cookies. She could try bribing him with Grandma's secret recipe to the World's Best Peanut Butter and Chocolate Chip Hip-Killing Cookies. Nicknamed the Evil Ones by the women in her family.

But all of her plans hinged on her surviving her current predicament, which given Joey now displayed numerous twitches, not just by the eyes but all over his body, seemed less and less likely.

"Would you stop your moaning?" he yelled at Miranda, not for the first time.

"Don't you yell at me, you pasty-faced lizard," she hollered right back. "It's not my fault junior here has the worst timing."

"It occurs to me," he snapped in reply, "that I don't need two hostages to draw the wolf and his friends here." He aimed his gun and thumbed the trigger.

"Don't you dare hurt them." Dawn stepped in

between Miranda and Joey. "She's innocent in all this, and so is her baby. Let them go. It's me you want."

The distraction worked. "Dear Dawn, so kind-hearted even when faced with annoying woodland creatures best served in a stew. For you, my sweet love, I will let the annoying rabbit live. But I'm done listening to her wailing. She stays here."

Not ideal, but better than Miranda getting killed. "Thank you." It galled Dawn to act gracious, but at this point, her only hope was to keep Joey calm long enough for help to arrive. If help was on the way. *I won't think like that. Everett and Chase, even Tom, are surely not far behind us.*

Dawn guided Miranda to a grassy spot and did her best to clear it of rocks and branches before spreading her jacket on the ground.

Miranda sank onto it and panted. "Darn it, Dawn. I wish I could help you."

"Don't give me a second thought. I'll be fine. You've got enough things to worry about. Starting with keeping calm and remembering your birthing classes and the breathing techniques to work through the labor pain."

"What classes? My plan was to have this sucker in the hospital drugged to the hilt with an epidural. I saw the movies on natural childbirth. The screaming. The blood. The gore. I might be tough, but I'm not a masochist!" Miranda grunted the last bit.

Patting Miranda's hand, Dawn couldn't exactly refute her claim, having also seen those videos and been present for a birth or two. She had nothing but the highest respect for those who chose to go the natural route without the drugs. She, on the other hand, would probably opt for the epidural, as she didn't do well with pain. She tried to offer reassurance. "I'm sure your husband will be along soon. He'll be able to help." If he didn't faint, a common occurrence among daddies.

"I know Chase will find me. He never lets me down. Just like Everett will find you." Miranda squeezed her hand before screaming, "Carrot-freaking-mother-of-all-cakes, that hurts!"

Dawn winced, less because of noise and more because Miranda practically crushed her hand. She hated leaving the bunny alone, but Joey was done being patient. Grabbing her roughly by the arm, he pulled her away from the cursing and sweating FUC agent.

"Good luck," she whispered, not knowing who needed it more at the moment.

Joey seemed to know exactly where he wanted to go, and with him partially dragging her, they eventually arrived in a ragged clearing bordered on one edge by a sheer drop-off. In other circumstances, the view would have proven magnificent; the trees on the far side a rainbow of fall colors, the striations of the rocky bluff an artist's dream.

"Where are we?" she asked as he released her.

"The wolf will recognize it. It's where he should have died the last time we met."

Remembering Everett's injuries, Dawn swallowed hard. The drop was steep and lined with rocks. Sharp rocks. It was a miracle he'd survived the fall the first time. Would he be so lucky a second? "You don't have to do this, Joey. There's still a chance for everyone to get out of this alive. Just turn yourself in."

"Never. I won't go back to a tiny cell. I won't let them tamper with my brain or take away my powers."

"Aren't you tired of hiding, though?"

"Once I kill those chasing us, I won't have to. We'll leave this place and start over, you and me, the happiest couple alive. Together, we'll make super babies. Just imagine them."

Unfortunately, she could. Ugly little critters with bulging eyes, four cloven hooves, and a nervous tic like Joey's. She'd rather die first.

How casually she accepted her probable demise. Then again, what else could she do? She'd already had plenty of time to analyze the situation. No matter which way she perused it, the end result was bleak. No way would Chase leave Miranda once he found her, which left only Everett and Tom to face the lizard menace, if Tom wasn't sent for help. If Tom ended up out of the picture, then that left a one-on-one. Psycho gecko against a cocky wolf. Who would prevail?

Dawn feared the answer.

24

ONCE EVERETT and his posse hit the woods, Chase shed his humanity in a burst that sent clothes scattering. He then proceeded to prove grizzlies could haul ass. Opting for four feet as well, Everett stuck close behind, ears perked, alert for any sound that might give him an indication of Dawn's status. As for Tom, he lumbered along behind in human form, clutching his beloved shotgun.

Fear of arriving too late made them reckless. They tore through the brush and undergrowth, making no attempt to mask the noise of their chase. Joey knew they were coming after him, so why bother wasting time with silence?

The acrid fear knotting his stomach was something Everett was unfamiliar with. Usually, he jumped into missions with all four feet and a cocky attitude, but this time, he wasn't fighting for himself or justice, but the woman he loved. *The woman I want as mate.* A future without Dawn just wasn't something he wanted to contemplate.

How strange to realize now as he tore through a forest at the heels of a bear that his father had spoken the truth when he said once you met the right woman, your life changed forever. Of course his exact words were, "Once I met the bitch, life as I knew it, as a free-swinging single man, was over." Not exactly a poetic sentiment, but still, Everett understood what he meant.

His perspective and goals in life had changed since meeting Dawn. The idea of settling down with one female, popping out cubs, and living a normal life, one not dependent on fast food, booze, and chaos, appealed to him. He wanted it. Wanted the normalcy, the passion they enjoyed together, the regular home-cooked meals that made him drool before he even sat down.

Would the fact he'd failed to protect her doom the dream before he got to have it?

Not if he could help it. He ran faster, outpacing the bear, straining for a sign, scent, anything to let him know they were closing in.

As it turned out, he didn't hear his little doe, but they all heard the sounds of a not-so-happy rabbit long before they reached her.

"I swear to the big carrot in the sky, I am going to sew my legs together when this is all over."

Someone was having last minute issues with the pregnancy it seemed. And she wasn't alone.

Ever see a massive grizzly slam to a sudden halt? It was a funny sight, especially given his momentum. Chase ended up skidding on his hairy ass and falling face first in front of his wife, who squatted over Dawn's coat that appeared soaked in some kind of fluid.

"About time you showed up," snarled the not-so-cute bunny in labor. "Here I am about to birth *your* child sporting *your* ginormous head while you're taking a leisurely jog through the woods."

"I got here as fast as I could," Chase growled right after he made a quick switch to his human form.

"I see someone needs to get his fat ass on a treadmill. Because that was not fast en—" Miranda didn't complete her harangue, probably because she was too busy screaming through her next contraction.

Arriving last, Tom already had his cellphone out and was calling their coordinates in to the furry coalition, requesting a doctor. Smart man.

"What can I do to help?" Chase asked.

"Other than neutering yourself?" Miranda panted. "Get ready to catch this sucker because junior is coming."

"Oh no it's not. You keep that baby in there. This is not the place or time to have our child," Chase commanded, his eyes so wide they practically popped out of his head.

"Keep it in? Ha!" Miranda laughed before yelling again.

Everett inched to the side, not wanting to be in the way of whatever came shooting out of the bunny's body. Unfortunately, his movement drew attention.

"You!" Miranda glared at him. "Why are you still here?"

"Um." Was there a correct answer that wouldn't piss her off?

Nope. "Don't just stand there like a slack-jawed idiot. That crazy freaking gecko has Dawn. You need to rescue her and kick his ugly lizard ass."

Everett glanced at Chase, who shrugged. "Go. I don't need your help with my wife. She's going to keep that baby in there until the doctor arrives."

"Ha. No, I'm not. But Everett needs to go. Now-OW! OW! OW!"

He didn't hesitate any longer. Off he sprinted, leaving behind a bellowing bunny about to give birth and a bear determined to not let her. As for Tom, who the fuck cared? Either he followed or he didn't. Dawn needed him.

It was with little surprise that Everett burst from the trees to find himself in the same spot he'd confronted the gecko before. Just one difference this time. Looking terrified, but uninjured, was Dawn.

Standing in his way, though, was a giant lizard. Just his luck, Joey was even uglier than before, slavering from his overlong teeth, his skin a scaly green, and his eyes rolling about madly inside his head, Everett wished he'd brought a gun so he could end this quickly. But, no, he thought he'd have a bear as backup this time and had foregone a weapon.

"Fee, fi, fo, fum, I smell lunch," lisped the gecko, his misshapen mouth straining to spit out the words.

"Wrong fairy tale, mosquito breath," Everett snarled before he shifted to his wolfman shape. Harder to retain because of the energy involved, he still opted for it, knowing from previous experience his wolf and human form were no match for the massive monster.

Just his luck, he'd lost his grizzly sidekick on the

way, not to mention Tom. He could have really used some help, especially from Tom's shotgun loaded with tranquilizer-coated silver shot.

A long tongue flicked from the reptilian face and slimed Dawn's cheek. Everett's wolf growled, a low rumble of discontent as she shuddered.

Joey took a lumbering step forward. "I think it's time we rewrote the stories. I'm sure people would love to read a tale about a wolf who gets his ass handed to him by a gecko."

"In your dreams, tailless."

"It'll grow back!"

"Maybe it will, but you'll still always have a small dick. Pity Mastermind couldn't fix that."

And with those fighting words, the battle was on.

Awooo!

25

Watching Everett battle with Joey was one of those moments of morbid fascination. On the one hand, she wanted to close her eyes and not see the violence and bloodshed. But, at the same time, a part of her wanted to help, to do something more than play the part of frightened spectator.

Not for the first time, she wished her father had encouraged her to learn how to defend herself, but he was an old-school buck who didn't believe females needed to learn how to fight. She lamented not doing something to teach herself once she'd left home. She so wanted to help Everett. Like a hero from a fairy tale, Everett had come to her rescue, his massive and gorgeous, sleek-furred lupine self morphing into a bipedal wolfman with massive teeth and claws. Towering taller than usual, he was impressive and vicious-looking. Against a normal shifter, she'd wager he would have proven virtually unstoppable. Against Joey with his drug-induced enhancements, though?

Even she, with her lack of experience, could tell her poor lover was losing.

Not that he seemed to notice or care. Snarling and snapping, Everett swung at Joey, claws extended. He ripped swathes of leathery skin, leaving deep, stomach-churning furrows, but in a berserker-type rage, the giant gecko didn't pay his wounds any mind. Joey meted out his own punishment, tearing his own strips of skin and fur from Everett. At one point, he even picked him up and tossed him hard into a tree trunk.

Dazed, Everett lay slumped at the base, groaning, which meant he was alive, but unable to stand. Joey ululated in triumph and stomped over, ready to mete out a final, deadly blow.

Just when it looked as though it was all over for her lover, Tom arrived to the rescue. With a crank of his shotgun, he fired at Joey, the silver shot pebbling Joey's body and halting his advance. Screaming in rage, Joey dropped to his knees. Tom cocked the weapon for a second shot and advanced on the fallen shifter.

Still recovering from his impromptu flight, Everett moaned and stirred, stunned but not down for the count. Joey hissed at the wolf. "I won't let you have her!" He struggled to his feet.

Tom took aim, but the gun didn't fire. "Not now," Tom grunted, hands yanking and pulling in an effort to unjam his shotgun.

Distracted, he didn't pay Joey any mind, and Dawn could only scream a warning, "Tom, watch out!"

He heeded her warning, his head rising to spot Joey lunging away from Everett toward him. He swung the shotgun as a club, but Joey proved faster and caught the long barrel in a clawed hand, ripping it free and tossing it to the side. Poor brave Tom, he tried to fight, but he was no match for the lizard. He must have sensed it because he tried to run, but Joey snagged him with his razor-tipped digits, puncturing flesh.

Dawn winced. Wrung her hands. Wished she could help. Do something.

You can.

Her subconscious prodded her. Reminded her that Joey wasn't the only changed one. How was that supposed to help her? *I don't know how to fight. What am I supposed to do?*

The answer was simple. *Anything I can. Whether it's in my nature or not, I need to do something, anything. I can't let them die.*

Shifting shapes was easy. Her doe had spent the last week or so since she'd taken up with Everett cooped up in her mind. Her other self bounded out with joy and an eagerness to join the fray that would have made Dawn cringe, but Dawn wasn't driving anymore.

Massive cloven hoofs pawed at the ground. Steam hissed from her nostrils. Her muscles twitched in anticipation. She lowered her crowned head, her antlers, an unnatural massive rack wider even than her father's, poised for battle.

She charged.

Whereas human Dawn saw her modified structure, namely the antlers on her head, as a horrible mutation that set her apart from all of her kind, her doe, the new version, who enjoyed a bit of blood sport and mayhem, reveled in them. The monster threatening her mate and his friend never saw her coming. But Tom did, judging by his wide eyes, as did Everett flanking the lizard on the side. Everett jumped away as she speared the lizard from behind.

Ooh the scream that came out of the mutated gecko. He dropped Tom to the ground and tried to reach behind him, but his stubby arms couldn't grasp anything. He remained skewered.

What should she do with him?

Finish him off. There was no saving him. His mind was too far gone. And she was in the perfect spot to end the nightmare. She drew on not just her enhanced musculature to lift the wretched lizard, but her telekinesis too. Higher and higher she raised her crowned head with the struggling gecko, the ichor dripping and rolling down her horns making her chuff as she pranced with her prize. The barbs on the tips of her antlers dug deeper the more her prey struggled.

The gecko morphed shapes, returning to his man form, still caught on her antlers, blood frothing at his lips.

"Why, Dawn? Why?" he croaked.

The proper answer was because Joey was a murdering monster who needed to be put down like a rabid animal. The real truth, though? *Because I love the wolf, and this abomination dared hurt him.*

With a mighty toss of her head, she flung the punctured body out over the abyss and watched as her foe bounced off the rocks before plunging into the raging river below.

There was one stalker who wouldn't be targeting any more women or campers.

"Holy shit."

Whirling, Dawn's blood-thirsty satisfaction shriveled as she beheld Everett's shocked expression as he hadn't just watched her kill a man, but also had beheld her mutant shape. Eep! What must he think?

Hurriedly, she thrust her doe back into the corner of her mind and morphed back to her human form, her nakedness the least of her concerns. But hiding her other shape couldn't make him forget what he'd seen.

She waited for him to turn away from her, to express his disgust in her less-than-perfect animal, to...

He enveloped her in a hug and lifted her feet off the ground as he swung her around. "Holy freaking shit, little doe. You were awesome!"

She blinked at his response. "I was?"

"Totally."

"You're not mad I killed him?"

"Mad? What on earth for? If you hadn't charged the bastard like you did, Tom and I would be the ones feeding the fishies. You saved us!"

"I guess I did." It slowly sank in that she'd not just defended herself, she'd fought back. She, a weak and fragile deer, according to her mother and father at least, had taken out a psychotic wanted criminal. The reality hit her in the knees, which folded, but thankfully, Everett was there to hold her up.

"I gotta say, I don't understand why you wouldn't show us your animal before."

"Isn't it obvious?" She was a freak of nature, a monster like Joey, just less inclined to killing people.

"Um, no. I mean, sure you were a tad more ferocious-looking than Bambi, what with the red eyes, giant hooves, and your somewhat larger than normal size, but, hey, at least you didn't have an extra tail or something."

"But I have antlers!"

He peered at her with puzzled eyes. "So? Don't most deer have them?"

"Not female ones. Male bucks have horns. Girls don't. Especially not gigantic ones like mine with sharp pointy barbs at the end."

"Really? Well, I'm sure glad you had them because they saved the day."

Didn't he grasp the problem? She explained it to him. "They're the reason I have to hide. Even from my family."

"Why? I don't see the big deal."

"It's the equivalent of being a bearded lady." Except, shaving wasn't an option. "If FUC knew I had them, they'd lock me up."

"I think you're making this too big of a deal. I mean, sure, maybe you look different from other deer, but that doesn't make you bad or evil. Heck, those horns saved the day."

Way to remind her. She just hoped the blood didn't permanently stain them.

"My family would have a heart attack if they saw."

"So don't show them. No one needs to know unless you choose to say something."

"You make it sound so easy."

"Because it is. Hey, even though all of the other reindeer made fun of Rudolph and his nose, eventually everyone came to love him, even Santa."

"You're not helping."

"Aw, come on, little doe. Give me a break. You know

I suck with pretty words. Does it help if I say that, horns or not, even the fact that your doe is bigger than my wolf doesn't make me love you any less?"

She resisted an urge to shove a finger in her ear and wiggle because she'd surely misunderstood. "Excuse me? What did you say?"

Everett coughed and peered at the sky then down at his scuffing toes. He cleared his throat, his discomfort palpable. "I, um—that is—oh damn it all. I love you, Dawn."

"You do?"

"Yes. Although this wasn't exactly how I pictured telling you."

"And how did you picture it?"

"For one, I wasn't bleeding like a damned stuck pig, and two, I was planning to have my cock inside you making you moan in incredible pleasure as I told you."

Romantic poetry would never be Everett's strong suit, but she'd not fallen in love with him because of his way of speaking. But was love enough? "You know we can't be together."

"Why not?"

"Because now my secret is out. I'm a mutant just like Joey."

"You're special."

"Exactly my point. What if FUC decides I'm a menace to society and decides to lock me up?"

"Then I'll bust you out, and we'll run away to Canada or Alaska. I don't care where so long as we're together. Although, I would prefer somewhere with cable. And beer. A wolf needs his necessities."

Why did she get the impression Everett wouldn't let

her walk away? *Because he loves me.* So why exactly was she arguing? She sighed. "You're crazy, and it must be contagious because, as it turns out, I love you too."

"Awooo!"

He howled in joy before swinging her around in his arms. "So that means you'll stay?"

"If FUC will let me, and—" she admonished before he could howl again, "if you patch things up with Tom."

"No patching needed," Tom stated as he arrived limping and bloody, but alive. "However, an apology is in order."

"I'm sorry," she promptly said.

"Not from you," he exclaimed. "From me. I've been acting like an ass."

"He gets that from his great-great-grandfather, who was a donkey," Everett interjected, while at the same time doing his best to keep her naked parts covered—using his own body, which was quite distracting.

Tom shook his head and stripped off his shirt, which despite its holes and blood, provided at least some attempt at modesty, something Dawn appreciated. As did Everett, who took her back in his arms for a normal hug instead of a shielding one.

"I judged you based on a piece of paper saying you were a criminal instead of who you were as a person. That was wrong of me."

"Hey, it's not your fault. According to FUC, I am dangerous. And, as we just saw, capable of hurting things."

"But only because you had to. You did more than most would have in a bad situation. You even stood up for me when I didn't deserve it. I misjudged you, Dawn, and for that, I'm sorry."

Leaving the circle of Everett's arms, Dawn went over to Tom and gave him a hug. Not a long one because a possessive growl let her know that a certain wolf didn't like it one bit.

"Oh give your dog a bone," Tom said to his friend. "I'm not stealing your woman, although I won't say the same for her cooking."

"You'll always have a place in our home and at our table."

"But no more sleeping on the couch," Everett added.

More talk had to wait because it was at that moment the cavalry arrived. A tough-looking dude sporting a FUC badge led the team from his perch atop a massive fox with giant golden orbs. When that freaky gaze turned their way, Everett took up a spot behind Dawn, as did Tom.

When she turned to peer at them over her shoulder, Everett shrugged. "Hey, I'm not too proud to let my vicious doe protect me from a giant vixen."

But Renee—who introduced herself later, along with Viktor and the rest of the team—wasn't interested in eating them, even if she could have with one gulp. She knelt down on the grass and peered over the edge of the cliff while Viktor, having first aid experience, patched Everett's and Tom's wounds. Not wanting to be in the way, and sensing a kindred spirit, Dawn stroked the fox's soft fur. She relaxed enough to finally remember to ask, "Hey, does anyone know if Miranda and the baby are okay?"

Viktor choked, and Renee chuffed, but it took a moment for Dawn to realize it was in mirth.

"Oh, don't worry about Miranda. When we came across them, Miranda was demanding we bring her some carrot cake, the baby was sleeping in her arms, and Chase was passed out face-first on the ground."

The laughter surrounded her in a warm wave, but not as hot as the hug she got when Everett clasped her in his arms after being pronounced fit to get in more trouble until a real doctor could assess him.

"What do you say we go home?" he whispered in her ear. "And we huff and puff our way to heaven."

"But what about your injuries?"

"You can tell me what a big booboo I have and kiss it better. And then I'll show you what a big di—"

She slapped her hand across his mouth. "Don't say it. Show me."

Unfortunately, the showing aspect took longer than expected. The medics insisted on patching Everett's various wounds, most of which had begun the healing process. The man possessed great genes—and not just the blue kind that hugged his perfect butt.

Once the doctor declared him in no immediate danger, they got waylaid some more. FUC needed answers. So off they trooped to Chase and Miranda's hotel room to Skype with Kloe, head of the nearest FUC office. Once they filed their reports on the takedown, filled in the paperwork for the bounty, oohed and awed over the new baby—lest Chase act upon his threat of ripping their arms off and beating them with them for not admiring the world's most perfect cub—and got a very drunk Tom home, it was late. Real late.

Dawn could barely keep her eyes open and kept yawning in a most unladylike manner. However, Everett didn't seem to mind. He stripped them both, his hands barely lingering on her flesh before he tucked her into bed, his body spooning against her back, his hand resting atop her tummy. It was comforting. Peaceful.

And so not what I want.

After the arduous day she'd spent, she couldn't deny her body needed rest, and Everett, despite the semi arousal pressing against her back, seemed willing to let her get it. But she didn't want to sleep. Not yet. Not when she'd come so close to losing him today. Not when she still stood a chance of losing him tomorrow if FUC decided to come after her. If this was their last night together, then she wanted something to remember. A last moment of pleasure.

She wiggled, a little jiggle of her bottom against his rigid shaft. It stiffened with interest, but Everett didn't get the hint because the rest of him didn't move.

Did he sleep? She squirmed again, and in case he didn't get her subtle hint, she placed her hand over the one splayed across her belly. She slid it up her ribcage until it cupped her breast. He squeezed and his lips nuzzled the back of her neck as he murmured, "What are you doing?"

"What do you think I'm doing?"

"You're tired. You should rest. It was a long day."

Yes, it was. And fatigue did pull at her, and probably him too. Was that why he didn't roll her over and do naughty things? Or were his injuries more serious and painful than he let on?

Suddenly, she felt bad. Perhaps his lack of interest

was because he fought to put on a stoic front. "Are you still hurting? Do you need some painkillers?"

"A little sore, but nothing I can't handle."

"Oh." She couldn't help the almost sigh of disappointment as she resigned herself to a night of sleep instead of the lovemaking she desired.

"Is something wrong, little doe?" He brushed his lips against her skin again, a light caress that sent shivers dancing down her spine.

"No."

His thumb stroked over her nipple, casually, with none of his usual sensual fervency. "Why do I get the impression you're not telling me the entire truth?"

"We should get some sleep."

"Is that what you want?" He tweaked her taut peak.

She made a sound. Should she lie? "No."

"Thank the full moon because holding back was killing me." He no sooner said that than she found herself on her back. His lips crushed hers in a kiss that stole her breath. Passion flared hot and fast. Her hands clutched at his head, her fingers tearing at his long strands, while he devoured her mouth, his tongue insistently weaving and sliding with hers. His hips undulated and dragged the head of his cock against her cleft. The hairs on his chest rubbed against her breasts, providing friction.

Dawn couldn't get enough of him. The taste of his mouth. The touch of his skin. The heat from his cock. The warmth and happiness being with him always brought.

Skin to skin, breath mingled and souls practically touching, they made love. They connected on a level she couldn't have explained in words but cherished with every ounce of her being.

Right here, right now, there was no fear or doubt about tomorrow. No worries. Just the two of them, rising on a tidal wave of bliss, a perfect storm of pleasure.

When he rolled to his back, she was ready for him, her sex drenched with desire, her body flushed with heat. His hands gripped her waist and steadied her as she angled herself to take him, the thrilling penetration of his shaft drawing forth a cry.

"Love me," she practically sobbed as she rode him, her body undulating atop his.

"Until my very last breath," he promised, his eyes staring into hers with an intensity that stole the last of her sanity.

Head thrown back, fingers digging into his chest, she let herself ride the wave of their passion into orgasm and dragged him with her. Together, they yelled their pleasure to the waxing moon high in the night sky. Their hearts raced in time, and mangled breaths huffed and puffed as their moment of ecstasy took them prisoner and cemented their bond of love and life.

The last of her energy spent, Dawn collapsed atop him and his arms came around her in a loose hug.

"I love you, Dawn." Such a simple statement, yet she could hear the sincerity in his words.

"I love you too," she murmured on the edge of sleep. *I love you so very, very much.*

A part of her still worried about tomorrow. Would FUC arrest her for being a mutant, or would they grant her clemency?

Only time would tell. No matter what happened, they'd find a way to be together. To carve their own happiness.

And if her greatest fear manifested and FUC came for her? She heard the Canadian Rockies were a nice place to hide.

Despite her anxiety over what the future held, it was nice to know the nightmare was over. Joey was dead. Everyone was safe. Even if it was for one night, Dawn could sleep and pretend she'd gotten her happily ever after with her big, bad wolf.

EPILOGUE

A FEW DAYS LATER...

IN THE END, IT TURNED OUT EVERETT DIDN'T NEED TO BUST her out of FUC jail, to his chagrin. Especially since he'd planned it all out and lamented more than once, *"What will I do with the stink bombs I bought? Pépé doesn't give refunds."*

Given her bravery in protecting Miranda and her baby, as well as her crucial role in getting rid of Joey, all outstanding warrants for Dawn were dropped so long as she agreed to let some FUC doctors keep an eye on her. She was a free-ranging doe again.

Everett rushed her home to celebrate, which meant they were both naked seconds after the door slammed shut.

Buried balls deep inside her, he finally gave in to his fantasy. He pinned her hands over head and thrust into her with long, sigh-inducing strokes.

DOE AND THE WOLF

"I," he murmured, sinking deep. "Love." He pulled out, teasing her with the tip. "You." Slam, he drove his dick back home.

Dawn's romantic reply. "Would you stop with the romantic stuff and screw me already?"

Laughing, he was only too glad to comply. Not so long ago, he'd thought the life of a lone wolf was all he'd ever want. Then he met his little doe. Now all he could think about was the future, a future where he didn't come home to an empty house, where he got fat eating excellent home-cooked meals, where he'd one day pass on his bountiful knowledge to his progeny—such as teaching his son how to write his name in the snow with pee. Heck, a sick part of him even looked forward to the day he got to threaten any boys who came sniffing around his daughters. *Don't make me eat you, boy!* But best of all, he loved knowing he'd get to spend the rest of his life with the woman he loved, waking up to her smile every day, her presence making his whole world a better, and happier, place.

Who said a wolf couldn't have a happily ever after? Point them in his direction. If they didn't believe him, he'd show them what big teeth he had right before he ate them.

Awooo!

(*The following needs to sung to the tune of Rudolph, the Red-Nosed Reindeer*)

You know Miranda and Jessie, Renee and

Clarice,
Chase and Mason, Viktor and Nolan,
But do you recall?
The most famous FUC agent of all?

Dawn, the mutant doe,
Had a very pointy rack,
And if you ever saw it,
I'd suggest you stand far back.

All of the other agents
Used to laugh and call her names;
They never let poor Dawn
Join in any FUC-ing games.

Once the mutant Joey got speared,
Kloe came to say,
Dawn with your rack so wide
We need you as an agent to fight.

Then how the shifters loved her
As they shouted out with glee,
Dawn, the big rack doe,
You'll go down in history.

Muahahahaha!

※

ELSEWHERE…

"Mom, look, there's a giant chicken with great big teeth chasing a man."

Nose buried in her garden as she weeded, the mother just said, "Sure there is, son." But while her boy and his fanciful imaginings were easy to ignore, the hollered, "How many times do I have to say I'm sorry?" caught her attention, but even in the short time it took to raise her head, the street was empty except for one large, drifting feather and a faintly echoing, "Squawk!"

The End…of this story but the fun continues in *Ostrich and the 'Roo.*

For more books, see EveLanglais.com

www.ingramcontent.com/pod-product-compliance
Lightning Source LLC
LaVergne TN
LVHW041634060526
838200LV00040B/1572